WET FEET

WET FEET

Sex, Life and Murder in the Caribbean

A Novel

B. D. Anderson

iUniverse, Inc.
New York Lincoln Shanghai

Wet Feet
Sex, Life and Murder in the Caribbean

iUniverse books may be ordered through booksellers or by contacting:

iUniverse
2021 Pine Lake Road, Suite 100
Lincoln, NE 68512
www.iuniverse.com
1-800-Authors (1-800-288-4677)

Because of the dynamic nature of the Internet, any Web addresses or links contained in this book may have changed since publication and may no longer be valid.

This is a work of fiction. All of the characters, names, incidents, organizations, and dialogue in this novel are either the products of the author's imagination or are used fictitiously.
All cover photographs by W. Anderson

Former Life Bar™ name and theme are trademarked by W. and D. Anderson

ISBN: 978-0-595-48608-3 (pbk)
ISBN: 978-0-595-60702-0 (ebk)

Printed in the United States of America

To the Memory of Michael A. Virga

"and there you have it."

CHAPTER 1

▼

ANGUILLA, ONE SPRING DAY

The British island of Anguilla is only a short trip across the channel from French St Martin. Inexpensive ferry service runs daily every half hour from Marigot's harbor to the Custom and Immigration station at Blowing Point. The quick 20 minute and very affordable ride brings many tourists and residents back and forth to work, for lunch, shopping or beaches depending on the need of the individuals. The mutual benefit to both foreign territories fosters the convenience and ease of movement. While Marigot is known for excellent shopping with French restaurants and bistros, Anguilla offers a slower pace with long stretches of fine white sand populated by fewer day tourists. On a normal workday, it can be a great escape for someone from St Martin who wants a quick change of scenery and less of a chance of running into friends or neighbors. Co-workers, Nat had promised Megan that they would enjoy a "real date" some day and today was the day.

As they exited the taxi on Shoal Bay beach, Megan grabbed both backpacks from the back seat as Nat paid for the trip and arranged for the driver to return 45 minutes before the last ferry of the day. The weather could not have been better for this early spring day. With a perfect temperature in the low 80's and a soft eastern breeze, the day was another wonderful gift of the Caribbean. Quickly surveying the beach, Nat selected a spot to the right and at least 600 feet from the only other couple in sight. Taking both backpacks from Megan, he motioned for her to walk first.

From behind her she heard, "You know I wanted to follow you so that I can see that fantastic ass move under your little sun dress."

Megan wiggled her rear end and turned back to look at him as she lifted the dress revealing a tanned butt with no underwear. "This one is for you, handsome."

"Stop that or I will trip over my hard on" grinned Nat playfully.

Megan's heart fluttered with happiness. As she approached the isolated spot he selected for them she reached and took one bag from him, opened it and pulled out two beach towels to spread on the sand. After arranging them side by side, she found a thong bikini bottom in the bag and slid it up her legs so that she could remove the dress. Nat sat on a towel and watched with joy as she stood in front of him wearing only the small sliver of cloth. Even though the Anguilla beaches do not allow topless sunbathing, Megan would not let British modesty ruin this moment. She stood still and felt his eyes explore her nearly naked body. Then she turned around for him twice as seductively as she knew how.

"Like what you see? Or are you simply lost in space?" teased Megan.

"Not bad for a first real date, darlin' ..." Nat answered. "And I haven't even offered you a joint or an adult beverage yet."

"What ever happened to dinner and a movie, damn it?" sighed Megan.

"Forget a movie on the beach, this trip! Unless you want to make one, Beautiful. For now I am off to scout out a bottle of cold chardonnay for us and possibly a perfect beach restaurant for lunch later. Once we have a buzz, of course" Nat said has he leaned over to kiss her and rub her bare shoulders.

"If you see any fresh fruit and bottled water, please bring that too with the wine. I brought some fancy plastic wine glasses, small plates, a cork screw and a sharp knife. This is going to be a great picnic breakfast."

Nat pulled off his polo shirt, kicked off his sandals and walked away in his bathing suit looking like every happy tourist on vacation. He turned to smile again at Megan and raised one hand with a stern gesture. "Hey, good lookin'. Don't pick up any rich old men while I am gone. You look like you just stepped off of one of those Mega Yachts in Simpson Bay Lagoon. You'd break my heart."

Megan dismissed him with a wide smile. "At least they would not leave me dying of thirst on Gilligan's Island for hours!" she laughed. "And don't forget my fresh fruit. I didn't have anything to eat this morning." As she stretched out her legs, Megan leaned back into the towel and enjoyed the warm sand beneath caress her back. Nat had only been gone for a few moments, yet already she missed him.

Nat returned with a soft pack cooler filled with ice, fruit, and wine. "I made friends with the bartender just down the beach. I told him that I had a high maintenance girl friend and needed to go first class for this day of sun and sand. Also I begged him for the cooler and explained that my sex life was depending on my ability to impress my date. He was quick to help. Of course, I also tipped him 20 bucks."

"You are amazing."

"Thank you. And you ain't so bad yourself. Of course, we'll probably get arrested for you being topless and we'll spend the rest of our youthful years in a British prison."

"Sounds like fun. I don't have any other plans" replied Megan as she turned over on her stomach in a self conscious move to hide her naked breasts.

Nat laughed and opened the first bottle of wine. Pouring a glass for Megan into her fancy beach wine glass, he made a show of twirling the glass and presenting it to her. "For my lovely ... you will also find two different Dutch cheeses in the container with your fruit. Enjoy!" He leaned forward once again and kissed her shoulders, neck, cheek then finally her lips. They held the kiss for a long time.

After half of the bottle of wine and most of the fruit and cheese was consumed, Nat stood and said, "It is time for a swim, my Mermaid." Lifting her off the sand he carried her to the water's edge with Megan holding on to his neck and enjoying the closeness of his bare chest as it rubbed against hers. As he waded into a depth over his waist, he gently lowered her into the sea but held on so that she could float on her back without effort. Then they swam and laughed with no purpose except to enjoy the clear water and find more opportunities to hold on to each other in the sea.

"Nat, do you think that I should get a boob job? I mean, if I ever have the money? I am so small."

"Darling, anything over a mouthful is wasted." replied Nat as he moved his face close to her breasts and brushed her nipples with his hand.

Pushing him away playfully, Megan dove under the water and pulled his swim trunks down to his ankles.

By noon, it was time for lunch. Megan put on her bikini top and Nat grabbed his polo shirt. Barefoot and holding hands, they strolled the long white beach towards the restaurants and hotels in no particular hurry. "Looks like the Beach Club with the friendly bartender will be our best choice. He is going to be pissed at us, however."

"Why?"

"I told him my hottie would dine topless today … how do you think I was able to borrow the soft pack cooler and get all that ice for our wine?" teased Nat. "I bet he has his digital camera ready! Now you are going to upset the poor guy."

She slapped him on the shoulder lightly. "Then email him my photo later. For now, I am starving! Let's get Grilled Lobster with garlic sauce!" Megan answered as she ran ahead and selected a table in the shade over looking the beach. Nat followed and waved to the man behind the bar as they approached.

Megan cocked her head to read the menu of drinks over the bar as she made herself comfortable in the seat. "Honey, can I have one of those frozen tropical smoothies with a funny little umbrella? It is time for a cool drink."

"What ever you want, my love." was his reply as he sat down and pulled his chair close to her.

Lunch went on for almost two hours. The local lobster was delicious and Nat ordered another bottle of wine once the two orders of frozen drinks refreshed and cooled them. Megan decorated the salt shaker with the silly paper umbrellas from the drinks. Not once did her current live-in boyfriend's name enter the conversation and it felt to Megan like they had left St Martin hundreds of miles away instead of just across the channel. A thirty something couple wearing bright new wedding bands and high style designer bathing suits took the table next to them and Nat was the first to welcome them and ask the obvious, "You guys on your Honeymoon?"

"Yeh," the young man quickly answered as he held hands with his new bride. "Do you come to Anguilla often on vacation? This is our first time. Family and friends recommended a condo villa to us on the beach and we really like it."

Nat answered. "Actually we live here. Well, not on this island but on St Martin across the channel. We just like to escape for a honeymoon reminder every now and then. We have been married for 3 years now. We like to visit this island whenever we can find time for a quick get-a-way on any three day weekend. You might see a movie star or two hanging around the private Villas on the major hotel properties." He wrapped his arm around Megan's shoulder and pulled her tightly to him.

"Wow, how romantic!" the new bride cooed. "You are both so lucky to live here. Do you have a house or an apartment?"

"We have an apartment in a house with a fantastic view, so it is the best of both worlds" answered Nat without skipping a beat. "Of course, my bride hates housework so we have to have a maid come in twice a week. The fringe benefits for me are worth it, I must admit." He turned and gave Megan a mischievous glance. She smiled back at him obviously enjoying his misrepresentation that they were a married couple.

When he started to add more to the story, Megan poked her arm into his side in mock protest, then took his hand and held it on the table. They both looked at each other's eyes for several seconds causing the visiting couple to shift their attention politely to the drinks that arrived at their table.

Then the waiter arrived with crème brulee for Megan and coconut pie topped with fresh strawberries for Nat. Both couples started more intimate and quiet conversations with each other and tuned out the surroundings. Nat drained his wine glass and poured more into his glass then topped off Megan's. He moved his leg to brush against hers and raised his glass in another toast. "Cheers, beautiful."

As they slowly savored the desserts and ate off of each other's plates, they were silent for several more minutes. Megan was the first to speak, "What you said to them … about us. It sounded wonderful, Nat. Even the crap about the house-keeper was sweet. Thank you."

"Listen here, Darling, at some point we will have to talk about where to live and how to live."

"Nat, what … what are you saying?"

"Together, I mean. I am talking about how we should live together. As in waking up together everyday" Nat responded without any hesitation.

"YES, YES, YES" was all that Megan could answer. Her bottom lip began to quiver and she felt light headed with joy.

Looking carefully at the expression of sincerity on the face of the man she loved, she squeezed her eyes tightly closed as tears welled up. Unable to completely pull her emotions together, she could only continue to whisper, "Yes, yes, yes." She had never been so happy or so surprised. *Days like today are what dreams are made of …*

"Megan, wake up" a female voice commanded. "You need to turn over so that you don't fry your skin on this side. You've been sleeping too long in this hot sun."

Megan opened her eyes and was surprised to see her friend Ingrid leaning over her in a bikini. Looking around, Megan realized that she was lying in the sand on Great Bay Beach in downtown St. Maarten. Several cruise ships were visible across the harbor. Music from the beach bars echoed up and down the area as excited visitors strolled the scenic palm treed bay. Stiff from the deep sleep, she rolled over and gave a disappointed look to her friend. "Oh shit."

"What's up with you, Girlfriend?" Ingrid asked with a soft smile. "You were sleeping so peacefully that I tried not to disturb you. But look at you. Another 15 minutes in this sun and you will need a burn specialist. Flip over and work the other side. I'll be right back with two cold beers and a fresh pack of cigarettes. You need anything else."

"How about a life?" moaned Megan.

"Okay, and I'll pick up a winning lottery ticket for you too while I am at it. See you in a minute" her friend shouted as she kicked sand with a slight run to the Philipsburg Boardwalk. Alone, Megan turned back toward the clear water and watched a stray beach dog saunter towards her. The dog paused for a hand out, sniffed about and then continued on its way when Megan failed to offer anything.

▼

CHAPTER 2

St. Martin, Wednesday, August 20

On the island of St. Martin early one Wednesday morning in August, Jack Donnelly woke to a bright blue sky with few white puffy clouds and a soft breeze across the protected water in the bay of Grand Case. With no curtains or shades on the wall of matching 6 foot French doors facing the beach, the room used the sun as an excellent alarm clock absent of annoying buzzes or blaring radio noise. Jack had been asking friends for years, "Why would anyone want to wake up to an obnoxious alarm or worse, a rude FM jock? The sun is all you need. Who the hell invented the alarm clock concept anyway? All we need is a little fresh air in the morning."

Once a sleepy fishing village, Grand Case had reinvented itself as the Gourmet Capital of the Caribbean with charming French restaurants located in old homes on the beach along both sides of the street to attract tourists and island residents everyday at lunch and dinner. There were few newer buildings. Most of the original structures were standing and were put to good use. Jack's apartment building was actually a large home divided into 4 apartment units with a small grocery on the street level. Parking was a nightmare and the street itself should have been made one way years ago because of the narrow size, but Jack was able to cope easily. "We are on an island. Who needs to go anywhere in a hurry?" he preached to the upset tourists who cursed the traffic at night.

Naked and rolling off the king size bed; he pulled on one of his favorite expensive French designer bathing suits and headed to the kitchen for a cup of coffee and a view of the sunrise as it cleared the mountains over the nearby hills wrapping around the bay. If only his police friends in New York knew this former fashion disaster was now wearing $100+ designer swimsuits, they would laugh until they peed in their uniforms. Jack's self defense excuse was simple, "If the suits are a favorite of renegades like that bad boy actor, Jack, then they are good enough for this Jack! Besides, they have a waterproof pocket for cash and my "keep dry" items like cash for the bar tab." *The mind can be a dangerous thing at times.*

Despite this being the height of hurricane season, the weather had remained the best in recent memory and the tropical winds lightly swayed the palm trees and lush plants around his rented apartment. "Stray Cat" met him at the terrace door for a bowl of Whiskas, a pat on the head, and an opportunity to lay around with human companionship after a hard night of hunting geckos. Jack, a retired New York City Detective, headed to the Caribbean almost 2 years ago to find solitude after the death of his wife, Catherine, from breast cancer. Somehow, he could never find the reason to return to living in the States. With family scattered around the country, no children, and a heavy heart, it just seemed better to spend more time looking at the beauty that nature offered. Jack had whittled down his responsibilities to paying the rent and bar tabs when due and feeding a feline friend who was consistent but undemanding. His sole purpose in life was to enjoy every day offered to him. In addition, this island had been friendly to him. The police on the Dutch side and the Gendarmes on the French side of the island quickly learned to enjoy and respect his brief visits, especially his newest friend J.R. Holiday, the Dutch side Chief Inspector. Forming friendships on this small island takes time; since local families go back for generations and most of the tourist population comes and goes with the regular swing of hotel and timeshare occupancies. J.R. Holiday, on the other hand, had asked for Jack's ideas for a media response just a month ago when CNN reporters showed up on the island regarding a recent multi-nation drug sting. Slowly, the experienced and resourceful former detective became an endless source of big city procedures and observations to help his new island friends and police colleagues. The only payment for services Jack required was a few beers while watching the sun drop behind the mountain over Great Bay in Philipsburg at the Get Wet Beach Bar. Technically undocumented as a resident on the island, Jack now understood the plight of Cubans, Mexicans, Haitians, and Chinese hiding in the USA and on many islands in hopes of starting a better life. His retirement checks, investments, and frequent trips off of the island offered some reinstatement of his tourist status but he was always walking on egg shells. At some point, he would have to apply for residency and hope for the best from his friends in law enforcement to put in a good word for him with the Lt. Governor.

Once Stray Cat was satisfied with a fresh bowl of dry food, Jack turned his attention to his coffee maker, decided to wait, then wandered slowly to the large bathroom in the center of the home. As he opened the door, Jack was momentarily surprised by two women's sun dresses draped over the towel racks and hamper. Looking at the freshly used towels on the floor and the other women's items on the sink, Jack reminded himself that he was not alone last night. With a quick smile, he made a mental note to ask Laura, the bartender at the restaurant bar next door, that his rum punches should have more fruit juice and less rum. Then turning to the mirror and seeing his chin in need of a shave, he shuddered. "Growing old ain't for sissies." He muttered under his breath, turned toward the toilet to relieved himself, and then lathered for a quick shave. Despite being in excellent physical shape for a 54 year old man, Jack's vanity made him wince when seeing the gray hairs that dominated his head. Somehow gray on the temples can be a dignified look, but too much gray in his hair and an unshaven morning beard made him feel like he should be washing the windows of cars waiting for the green at stop lights in New York City and asking for a dollar.

Once back in the kitchen, Jack filled the coffee machine with water and scooped 5 generous portions of Dominican coffee into the filter. As the machine popped away with the fresh brew of the morning the sound of laughter came from the deck stairs as two 40 something and obviously naked women entered the terrace with wet hair, towels waving in the air, and smiles of mischief.

"Hey Jack! Cheryl and I were wondering if you would wake up early. We need to return to the hotel before the family and friends call to check on us. That's the problem with just needing to get away from the kids and ex.-husbands. For women traveling without men, everyone thinks you are basically helpless. Worse, two women traveling together have two times the coverage of concerns from family. Our hotel room phone will start ringing off the hook by 8 AM. Did you sleep well?"

"When finally allowed to sleep, I slept like a rock." replied Jack. "But I'm feeling like I may have lost my virginity to you two."

Both women looked at each other and giggled like school girls. Just steps from Jack and the kitchen, Cheryl continued to dry her long blond hair while Susan, a slightly heavy but shapely red head, maintained a degree of modesty by wrapping her towel around her body as she sat down. "We hope that we did not upset your neighbors swimming naked this morning. No one was around and you are a bit light on women's clothing. You don't mind that we borrowed some of your large beach towels, do you Jack?"

"Not at all, the beach is topless and many of the European beach goers even change clothes completely on the beach. Plus it's still early. No tourists with cameras in the restaurants to grab a quick shot of you with a telephoto lens and publish it on the internet. Would you like some coffee? It's fresh, but I don't have cream or sugar in the apartment." In the bright morning sun Jack could not help noticing that Cheryl did not dye her hair. Or she paid close attention to detail.

"Oh shit! We forgot about photos on the internet. Did you take some, Jack?"

"I will if you have a few hours to spare" nodded Jack.

"Sounds like great fun, Jack! Maybe later this week! For now, we need to get back to the hotel for those family phone calls. Besides the morning's Brunch is starting early today … the hotel promised endless bloody marys, fresh seafood crepes and some soft jazz from a live group. What could be better on a day like this? Will you join us later or just come with us now?"

Jack considered going with them now, but paused to avoid rushing this rather wild and unlikely new relationship. "Possibly. You never know what pleasures the day can bring in Paradise."

The women turned to look at each other and burst into laughter again. Susan tiptoed close to Jack and placed her arms around his neck. "Dear Jack, do you realize that if either of us had been alone at that bar last night and met you nothing would have happened? Especially with the wedding ring you wear. But when the two of us started talking to you and heard about your wife, I don't know. We suddenly couldn't help ourselves. What do they say in Vegas? What happens in Vegas …"

"Ouch. I thought that you ladies were attracted to my boyish good looks. Or that you confused me with a wealthy move star" Jack said with a feigned look of rejection.

"Jack, don't be pensive for goodness sakes. Susan and I are here to have fun, act crazy, and leave the normal boring life behind for a few days. Do you think we go topless on the Jersey shore?" chimed in Cheryl. "Besides, when you admitted that you had not had sex since your wife died, we could not help ourselves. Consider our night together was needed therapy for you with two physical treatment specialists."

"Thank you, Doctors" replied Jack with some sincerity mixed with a slight feeling of guilt. "Good thing I never attended Catholic schools growing up. You two might have driven me into counseling."

Both women fired back immediately, "Oh sure."

As they leaned forward to him, Cheryl and Susan simultaneously kissed Jack on the cheeks then headed directly to the bathroom with their towels once again held high. Enjoying the view of the mature and slightly heavy women as they skipped away naked, Jack grabbed a full cup of coffee and with the cat trotting behind him, he headed for the terrace. Sitting down on one of his favorite wicker chairs with a full view of the sea, he somehow felt younger than he did on most mornings. Smiling to himself, he looked across the water to nearby Anguilla and whispered, "So it wasn't just a dream."

Within five minutes, their voices behind him once again caught his attention. "We hope to see you later, Jack! We're headed to Club Orient for an all over tan after the brunch. Bring that cute butt of yours to the beach if you don't make it to the hotel for food." Cheryl yelled as the front door opened and closed. Jack could hear more laughter as they strutted away. Meeting those two last night at the bar next door to Jack's condo building was not exactly in his plans for the evening but he certainly did not consider the experience unpleasant, especially for a widower who desperately missed the touch and scent of a woman. Now, he found himself whistling the silly "double your fun" chewing gum commercial. *Was that from the 60's or 70's?*

With his guests gone, the silence of living alone returned to the small home. The surf continued to lap softly on the sand and Jack watched the water ripple as an occasional pelican dove for a morning treat. Since it was still before 7 AM, the early sparkling sun gave the water colors that dazzled his eyes.

Stray Cat rubbed against Jack's foot as he sat by his chair as he did every morning. The coffee was already giving Jack the usual wake up call of caffeine when the cell phone in the kitchen started playing, "Take me out to the Ball Game." Standing and reaching for the phone before the next repetitive verse, Jack was careful not to step on the little guy.

"Good Morning, this is Jack."

In the Caribbean, good morning and good afternoon are considered polite and necessary before any communication. Even when entering a crowded room of strangers, it is polite. Many tourists jump into a conversation and are immediately viewed as rude by local people. "What time is my flight?" is rarely met with immediate customer service or a smile in the islands. Living and adjusting to island time behavior, Jack had learned to love the culture and customs. He waited for a voice on the other end of the phone call to reply in like fashion.

"Good Morning, Jack. This is J.R.; I hope that I did not wake you too early."

From the time the two men first met while watching jets land and take off at the Sunset Beach Bar just a few feet from the airport runway, they often called either other from time to time to touch base and plan another Sunday trip to watch the large air bus planes from Air France taking off with ear splitting thunder a few feet way from the road and the well known beach bar. The real show, however, was not actually the jet itself as it took off. Instead, entertainment was provided by crazy thrill seeking tourists who hung by their arms on to the chain link security fence. Often the brave spectators' legs were blown into the air by the jet blasts as they held on and screamed with delight. Jack considered it one of the stupidest acts that he had ever witnessed. But the beer was always cold and the scenery was outstanding.

"No, not at all. I was just finishing my first cup of coffee and enjoying this perfect morning. How are things with St. Maarten's best Inspector and protector of the peace?"

"Just listen. I hate to ruin anyone's perfect morning, but I need you at the beach on the French side where they found a body earlier today. I've heard from some scattered phone calls that the car with the possible murder victim has Dutch side license tags and that the French Gendarmes want us involved immediately. There have been several sporadic reports from the first officers on the scene … white guy, no ID, no keys in the car and of course, no money in his pockets. This is not good. Everyone is worried that a tourist was robbed and killed. The Lt. Governor wants answers and wants them fast. I was hoping that you could help once again."

CHAPTER 3

▼

JUNE OF THAT YEAR

Earlier that summer, Conrad and Megan sat at the Get Wet Bar on Philipsburg's newly built waterfront board walk relaxing with a few drinks after work with Nat, her boss. Nat dominated the conversation with stories of old girlfriends, sailing trips to St. Barts, and dumb co-workers from his past employment confrontations. Everyone he had been forced to deal with in business was a "fucking idiot", and no one could ever appreciate his cleverness or genius in decisions. Nat was indeed a legend in his own mind. Once on another island, he had outsmarted his boss only to be ejected from the job when she found out that he was accessing her employee files without permission. He was a clever guy, for sure. At another time and another company, he took company petty cash money from the desk of a co-worker and then accused the man of not following established procedures of locking the desk. The poor co-worker nearly freaked out over the loss of the money then was further humiliated when Nat revealed the prank in front of others. Whatever happened, no one was as smart as Nat. As the drinks flowed, his tongue continued to wag. He told of taking a job as a waiter back in the states in his younger years and being asked to leave on the second night. "Fucking assholes. Fucking idiots." They were everywhere and he seemed to find them and always out smart them.

Conrad noticed the gleam in Megan's eyes as she watched her boss and agreed with his pronouncements. Often smiling at his stories and alcohol induced wisdom; Megan leaned closely and touched his arm with hers on the table. Nat's chain smoking and continuous hand movements when talking were accentuated by the large diamond earring in his left ear he flashed as he turned his head constantly from side to side. It seemed that Megan was completely entertained. It was more than Conrad could stand. Despite the low lighting, Conrad could see the inches between them grow smaller and he wondered where Megan's legs were located under the table. He reached over and held her hand closest to his side of the table and mentally tried to pull her body away from Nat. She ignored the overture and continued to focus on the story teller. Thankfully, a young French man hurried up and greeted the group. Conrad welcomed the interruption of Nat's performance. Bored by Nat's voice, his eyes had started to glaze over. Nat introduced the new arrival as Philippe, a friend from Martinique. After kissing Megan on both cheeks in the classic French custom and shaking hands with Conrad, he joined the group with a bottle of Heineken in hand and sat next to Nat.

The break was a short one. Nat immediately took center stage to begin another tiresome monologue now that his audience had increased by one. After another 45 minutes of continuous war stories, Conrad had had enough. "Sorry Nat, this is great but Megan and I need to get home early. Tomorrow is a school day and we are half drunk already." announced Conrad as he stood. "Can I pay for our portion of the check?"

"Just leave a ten. I'll get the rest." was the reply. "Besides, you are taking my girl." Nat smirked then followed with a forced laugh.

His single laugh then turned into a girlish giggle accented by more arm movements and shaking shoulders. His bobbing head and repeated chuckles rubbed Conrad's nerves raw.

As his faced reddened, Conrad stood silently for a moment, then reached into his khaki pants and pulled out some money. Grabbing a twenty, he dropped it on the table and pulled Megan away from the men. Within seconds they were gone.

Philippe looked at Nat, then moved closer and said, "He doesn't think you are fucking his girlfriend too, does he?"

"I don't give a rat's ass what he thinks. He's a fucking idiot. Did you bring any grass?"

As they marched too quickly home from the bar, Megan shook off Conrad's hand and followed him back to the apartment they shared a few blocks away. Both moved silently and avoided any discussion of Nat's comment. As they approached the building, Conrad pulled out a key to the door, opened it and stomped up the narrow stairway in front of Megan leaving her to pull the door closed. She closed and locked the door. She stood alone for a few moments in the small foyer space, and then followed him up and into the 2nd floor apartment.

She heard him enter the bathroom and start to urinate. "I had to pee like a race horse, but was afraid to leave you alone with your boy friend. You two are very cozy, if you ask me. I thought if I left you long enough you would be under the table sucking his dick."

Embarrassed and angry, Megan said nothing. She entered the small living room area and turned on a table lamp as Conrad returned from the bathroom and laid down on the sofa, "Get me a beer, okay?" She turned and slowly shuffled around the open counter separating the living room from the efficiency kitchen and pulled on the refrigerator door. Popping open a beer and adding a cut lime from a dish on the top shelf, she reached for a recently opened wine bottle and removed the cork. As she turned, Conrad brushed her back with his chest and hugged her to his body. She stood still for a moment and felt his hands pulling up her sundress. She closed her eyes and enjoyed the movements of his hands up and down the sides of her back and across her breasts. Placing the wine bottle and the beer on the counter, she braced her hands on the counter and started to moan with pleasure. He kissed her back, her breasts, and finally her mouth. Then shutting the refrigerator door, he lifted her on to the counter and removed her thong underwear. She was not wearing a bra. With her dress still pulled up to her neck, he bent her back on the counter and poured beer into her naval. Licking the liquid before it ran off her body, he moved his mouth down to her pubic area and started to kiss and flick his tongue as she responded with moans and cries. She bent her legs and pulled her knees into the air as she grabbed his hair and pushed her pelvis even harder into his face. Shaking from the orgasm, she released him.

Conrad whispered, "Nice body shot. Your turn."

Megan slid off the counter as Conrad dropped his pants to the floor and swung up to replace her on the bar. She poured some wine into her hands and gently rubbed his growing erection. "Ahhh ... that's cold." Conrad said in mock protest.

"And you think your beer on my belly wasn't cold?" she said as she licked the wine from his penis.

Leaning back, Conrad propped himself on both elbows to better see Megan take him into her mouth, then grabbed the dress now curled around her neck and pulled her head up. "Time to move to higher ground baby." Pulling her into the living room by the twisted dress like a leash, Conrad placed her on the sofa face down and spread her legs. With one knee on the sofa and the other leg braced on the floor, he used his left hand to hold the dress snuggly and the right hand to rub between her legs.

"Ouch. Easy, Conrad the Barbarian. Please take the dress off me. I can't concentrate. You are pulling too hard. My neck hurts."

Conrad pulled the dress up and over her head. He grabbed her hips and positioned her on her knees while still behind her. Shifting slightly, he dropped her dress on the floor and opened the drawer on the coffee table with his left hand. She heard him as he moved some items around inside obviously searching for something. When he found what he was looking for, he pulled it out and shifted back. Megan kept her head down and started moving her pelvis seductively. His right hand continued to rub between her legs. Then he removed his hand and grabbed his penis. He rubbed the head up and down her ass and used her arousal from the last orgasm to wet the tip.

"That's a real cock on your ass, Babe. Not just a little needle dick like your bug fucking boss" he said forcefully.

"Honey, I never fucked him."

"And you never will" he snarled as he hit her buttocks with his erection.

Feeling his penis almost enter her, she moaned softly. He pushed his erection against her again without penetration. She expected to hear the mild hum of a vibrator but all remained silent behind her. Then she sensed the cool surface of hard metal next to her face. Gazing to her left, she saw a small gun in Conrad's other hand pointed at her.

Totally caught off guard, she thought, "*What the hell? Where did this gun come from?*" Speechless she gasped, hopping that she would not pee on the furniture.

He entered her and began the rhythm of intercourse while holding the gun inches from her head. Wide eyed, Megan responded to his movements while she stared at the gun in fear. Oddly she noticed her own desire quicken and so she reached to her pubic area with her right hand and began to rub herself in time with his motions.

He slapped her butt hard and the unexpected loud pop of his hand on her bare skin sent a rush of adrenaline through her body. Astonished by the amount of wetness between her legs, she started to moan "Yes, yes, yes."

Leaning his head close to her ear, he began to breathe heavily with sexual excitement. Then he quickened his thrusts. "Come on baby. You want me to shoot. You want me to shoot off now."

Megan rubbed herself harder and let the flood of his climax blend with hers.

CHAPTER 4

▼

EARLY TUESDAY NIGHT, AUGUST 19

The Greenhouse Restaurant located near the ferry dock for the cruise ship visitors in Philipsburg always rocks, especially on Tuesday nights. "Two for Tuesday" means drink specials, lots of locals and tourists, and the pool tables remain busy all night. Nat, an expatriate with a tourist retail business on Front Street, was clearly in command of the pool table. While others played with skill and a good degree of luck, Nat could see the geometric patterns and played with confidence and ease. Probably the result of a misspent childhood, it was now a great way to entertain the bar crowd while pumping up his male masculinity and image in the late night community.

"Hey mon, watcha doin?" his opponent yelled as Nat moved quickly to clean the table after the break. Nat shrugged, paused and then missed the next shot. Quickly, the local man moved in to shoot and recover the previous loss suffered. However, after three good judgments on angle and position, the beer and the ego over took the ability of the young challenger. The opportunity to win returned to Nat and he used it to his advantage. As he caught the eye of a large man standing in the corner, Nat quickly swept the table and crushed the chances of the opposition. Nat scanned the crowd after the victory. The large man acknowledged and gave a quick motion of recognition.

Megan, a frequent visitor to this popular neighbor bar, beamed as Nat moved from the tables and sauntered over to her. Even though she lived with Conrad, Megan had hoped for something romantic and permanent to develop with Nat to offer her a new life. She and her boyfriend lived from paycheck to paycheck, rarely went out for a nice dinner, and spent too much money getting high and drinking into the late hours of the night. Now over 30 with the biological clock screaming, it was time to stop the party and find a partner for life. Children would be nice, but security would be better. To her, Nat had it all and he was interested in her. It started like a junior high school episode of brushing against each other in the stock room and recently escalated to him asking her to meet for drinks on a regular basis. When she needed a ride home after an office Happy Hour celebration, he grabbed her butt as she entered his car so she rubbed him on his shoulder and arms as he drove through the slow pace of traffic to her apartment. While he never really suggested any relationship, she assumed Nat's reluctance was the result of her boyfriend as an issue and that Nat was being a gentleman. But all of the touching and attention could not be by accident. In the car that first time, she made it clear that for her an intimate relationship was welcome. Away from traffic, she unzipped his jeans and put her head down. Nat pulled the car off the road and released the seat to the furthest back position. It was quick and awkward. Neither of them made any comments after the encounter or the next day in the store. Since then the episode had been repeated many times in the store after closing, and always without affection for her. Once he turned her around, pulled up her sun dress and started to play with her ass but quickly moved back in front of her and pushed her into a knelling position for his pleasure. Megan was frustrated by the lack of romance but rationalized by thinking that he just needed more time to be sure before taking the next step. Earlier that summer, after a trip to the airport to pick up a delivery of new stock they rode out to LeGalion Beach to steal an afternoon together. They parked his car in an isolated area that Nat called his favorite, drank wine and smoked pot. When Megan felt a buzz coming on, she was sure that they would have sexual intercourse for the first time. Unfortunately the time passed quickly, and they needed to return to town before anyone especially Conrad missed them. She ended up giving him another blow job during the ride back to town to keep him happy and she hoped, interested. Later, she realized that they had never even kissed.

"Hey Babe" Nat announced as he moved closer to her at the bar. "Thanks for coming to see me play. Where is your boyfriend, Guard Dog, tonight? I hope that we can play without him for a while. I don't think he trusts me!"

"Not to worry. He has to supervise inventory of three stores tonight and the team can rarely finish before 11 o'clock. Then he always goes out drinking with the boys, so I am free to spend some time. My cell phone is off. What did you have in mind, Boss?"

Placing his arms over her shoulders and grabbing her back at the bare point under her short top, Nat smiled and turned in what was obviously a show for the crowd. Megan was well known. Her English accent was always charming to the men. She projected happiness. She partied hard but never was sloppy. Megan never wore a bra. Her firm breasts, perky nipples, and small body size displayed by tight clothes created a lot of interest from guys in the resort community. It was no surprise that a lot of men hit on Megan, but none were able to touch. She had been around the block and knew how to shut down the most aggressive drunk, horny tourist whose wife was off shopping or any local stud regardless of the amount of gold chains or charm. But now Nat was in. And everyone knew it. The music was loud, the drinks were flowing, and the air was filled with sexual tension.

Megan excused herself for a quick trip to the bathroom and left Nat at the bar watching the other pool players as the crowd grew and the music continued. Quickly, the large dark man who gave Nat the acknowledgement during the pool game slipped beside him on a bar stool. Both men looked at each other confidently and greeted with a pseudo handshake of clenched fists lightly bumping each other.

"You beat da last one, but only 'cause he gave you anuder chance. He be drinking fast and showing off" the large man said as he turned to watch the next pool game that started just beyond Nat's back.

Nat noticed several healing scars on the big man's shaved head. "Shit, T-man. He's a fucking amateur. A fucking asshole. I missed after the breakshot on purpose to give the loser a chance. I never had to worry about his silly ass winning" replied Nat with a tough guy scowl.

The big man remained silent. After looking around to make sure no one could hear, he lowered his voice and growled, "I came for da rest o' da money."

Nat leaned forward and dropped his voice, "What a joke. You think there is something that I don't know? What do you think I am? A fucking mushroom? You want to keep me in the dark and feed me shit. I'm real tired of this bull shit and I won't take it anymore. If you and your friend don't do better, I'll find someone who will. Who do you think you are fucking with? I pay for the boat so you can make lots of quick cash. I ask for you to scare some idiots and you fuck it up. If I know you, the problem was caused because you had your dick in your hand instead of following my instructions. You and Whip are fuck ups. You get nothing more for that fucked up job you did. Now leave me alone."

The large man spun slightly with a menacing motion and raised the corner of his shirt revealing a handgun in his waist band. "You gonna see me again." He snarled as he stomped quickly into the dark of night. As he hurried past some empty tables on the edge of the parking lot, he kicked a chair into the air. Yelling out loud, "T-man don't take dis shit from no man!"

When Megan returned from the bathroom refreshed and smiling, she found the place at the bar where she left Nat empty. A small amount of cash for the tab lay in the water from the last round's beer bottle sweat. She scanned the room but did not see him anywhere. She sat down, lit a cigarette and turned her cell phone back on. When she caught the eye of the bartender, he quickly turned away.

With a sigh, Megan collected her purse and phone and strolled outside. At the end of the parking lot she saw two slender white men both in jeans and wearing casual shirts. She immediately recognized Nat and Philippe, a younger French guy that was probably Nat's closest friend on the island. Nat was handing him a Heineken bottle and they toasted with a click. Megan stepped into the shadows and watched without making a sound. The two men stepped even closer together and talked. After a few words and some laughter, Philippe turned and pointed towards the alley leading to the Casino. Standing in the shadows and waiting were two young women, both blond and dressed in short, silky "Fuck me" outfits complete with 4 inch spike heels. *Eastern European escorts paid by the hour, I am sure. Both are probably illegal as hell and just here for some quick money.* Megan thought. Philippe motioned to them to walk toward Nat's SUV and then all four of them got into the car. Oddly, Philippe joined Nat in the front passenger seat and the girls entered the back seat through one door. The car started and rolled out of the parking lot toward Front Street then disappeared from Megan's view. Alone and even more disappointed, Megan reached in her purse and pulled out a cigarette. She noticed the keys to Conrad's car with her lipstick and momentarily debated following to see what Nat and Philippe were doing tonight.

"Damn you Nat" left her mouth with the next exhale of cigarette smoke.

Turning back towards the busy restaurant, she quickly decided to return to the bar and get a drink. Nat had not even offered while he was there, she realized. As she reentered the main dining floor to cross to the bar, two rather heavy men sitting at a table in the corner by the door looked at her, stood briefly and waved her over.

"Hey Good Lookin' … you want to have a drink with us? My friend, Vinnie, here fell in love with you when you were at the bar with that skinny dude and damn near died of a broken heart when you followed the asshole out of this place" said the fatter man as he flashed a heavy gold chain, gold bracelets and gold watch with every animated movement.

"Where are your wives?" asked Megan as she noticed wedding bands on both men.

"Back home in New Jersey with their boyfriends, I'm sure" replied Vinnie as both men laughed a little too loudly. "We are jewelry salesmen from New York and come to call on the Front Street stores."

Megan was not impressed. "How cute. You travel together."

"Damn right, lady. Ever since that jewelry salesman was murdered in mid-afternoon walking down the street with his sample case our company requires two men to travel for safety" replied the guy wearing the most gold. "By the way, I'm Michael. What's your name, Sexy?" He leaned forward and Megan could smell too much cologne.

Megan suddenly remembered the horrible murder just two blocks away last year and was embarrassed by her own callousness. "I'm Megan. I suppose that if you are buying, I can sit for a short time. You need to know that my boyfriend is working around the corner and could come in at any time. He is bigger than you guys, jealous, and violent at times if he sees me talking to strange men."

Michael looked at Vinnie and winked so that Megan could not see his reaction. He was not buying the big boyfriend story for a minute. He had seen Nat's little show of ownership of this broad. Then he had witnessed Nat's quick departure and Megan's chase after him. *What a lying slut. Yeh, there is probably some stupid boyfriend sitting at home waiting for her to return from the fucking library. This Bitch is looking for someone with some cash to spend on her and a good fuck. Let's do it.*

As Megan took the seat they offered between them, she noticed the waiter headed to the table with more USA domestic beers for them and her favorite tequila shots already poured. Two for Tuesday meant double drinks so each man received 2 beers on every order and Megan was given 4 shots. The waiter put the drinks down without comment and cleared 8 empty bottles from the table. It was obvious from the sound of their voices that Michael and Vinnie had been in the bar for a while.

Michael leaned into Megan. "You English? I love that accent of yours …"

Megan had heard this line before. "No, I'm from South Africa."

"Well, damn then. Here's to sexy accents from down under" said Vinnie.

Megan kept her mouth shut. *So much for a basic understanding of world geography for these two assholes. Now they think I am from Australia.*

Everyone toasted and Megan drained 3 of the shots before she caught herself and slowed down. *Damn I needed that, thanks to you, Nat.*

"So it sounds like you live here with that great big mean boyfriend of yours..what did you say his name was … Arnold Something or Conan the Barbarian?" asked Vinnie as he moved his shoulder closer to Megan and placed his leg against hers. "You are one hot number, that's for sure."

Close but no cigar, damn, what if he does know Conrad's name? No, that was just a coincidence. Megan pulled back to release contact with Vinnie's leg but only found herself pushing her shoulder against Michael. They were making a sandwich of her. "No, my boyfriend's name is Jonathan. She realized that the connection of these men to Conrad's employment could cause her some problems. *Sitting down with these two pigs was not a good idea.* Just as she started to excuse herself and stand the damn waiter appeared with another round and 4 more shots for her. *Shit. When it rains, it pours.* Megan downed two more shots and sat back to discover that Vinnie's arm had moved behind her chair. *Do these slobs think that I am attracted to either of them? Shit.*

In an effort to move away from the men and grab another shot, Megan dipped forward enough that one of her spaghetti straps slipped off her shoulder and showed too much cleavage. Michael's head almost bumped her chin as he leaned into her chest to look down her top.

"Tea cup titties! Love 'em!" the fat man slobbered without moving his head away. "So you like big men, huh?" Then he slid his hand up her cotton athletic shorts and wedged his fingers under her panties on the outside of her hip. "We got some nice jewelry for you in our sample case back in our hotel room, don't we Vinnie? You just need to be good to us and be a very bad girl." His breath was heavy and sour with beer.

Megan froze. Making a scene in this neighborhood hangout would cause a real fall out tomorrow with Conrad. So far the low lighting and the placement of their table in the far corner prevented anyone from noticing that she was being felt up by Michael. Plus Vinnie was so close to her body that his large frame was hiding the groping from the line of sight of the bar crowd. *Thank goodness for little favors. I need to get the hell out of here and fast.* She stood and jerked the hand from under her shorts in one movement and announced, "I have to pee. Be back in a moment, guys." Stepping from around the table with her purse she turned toward the parking lot and Front Street. In a split second she was out the door and moving away from the lights.

Vinnie stood. "Fuck! The Bitch is bolting on us. The damn bathrooms are in the other direction. I'll get her back, or knock the shit out of her and fuck her in an alley."

With a hundred feet or so from her to the restaurant, Megan looked back only to see Vinnie leaving the exit in pursuit. *Now this really sucks.* She picked up her pace but was reluctant to break into a run with so many people walking on the street. She knew her apartment was only a few blocks away and most of the street was well lighted. If she could just find the keys in her purse now, she might have a chance to open her door and lock it before Vinnie reached her. *Where are those keys?* Her pulse quickened as she dug her hand around in the bottom of the bag without success. Almost running now that she was away from stores and entering Back Street to her apartment alley, she stopped under the last street light before reaching her entrance and started tearing through the junk in her purse. Vinnie's footsteps became audible and she panicked. As she ran to the door, she found the keys and fumbled to find the right one. Vinnie was close and was running towards her. When he reached less than 20 feet from her, she pushed the door open. Letting it slam against the wall and remain open, she left the keys in the lock and hurried up the stairs taking two at a time. Throwing her purse down in the living room she opened the drawer next to the sofa and pulled out the small revolver. She could hear Vinnie walking up the wooden steps slowly obviously unsure of what might be at the top.

Looking down the narrow stair well, she raised the gun and reached for a light switch. "Stop where you are, asshole." The light at the bottom illuminated him perfectly.

Vinnie was completely caught off guard by a gun in the hands of his lust target. He immediately stopped and gave her a look of surprise. "What the fuck? Are you crazy? We just were trying to have a little fun. Put the gun down. Let's not do anything stupid here."

"The only thing stupid here is when two fat slobs from the suburbs think they can buy sex with me for a few pieces of cheap jewelry and some half priced shots of tequila."

Vinnie took a step up and said, "Come on girl, put the gun down. You don't want to shoot anyone. Let's try starting this night over."

It may have been the alcohol, it may have been the disappointment, it may have been the constant harassment she endured from men, but now Megan saw Nat, Conrad, and some obnoxious stranger all in one standing on her steps wanting to hurt her. The anger rose like a tsunami wave. She pulled back the hammer of the revolver and lowered her voice as she growled, "Not only do I want to shoot this gun but I am going to enjoy it."

"Come on now. Come on. It was that asshole Michael feeling you up. Don't shoot me, I'm your friend. Shit, lady, I just followed you to apologize."

Megan responded with a drunken and evil smile. Then her face contorted with anger as she said, "Goodbye."

"Fuck lady. You're one crazy bitch."

Silently, Megan started down the steps.

Finally sensing real danger, Vinnie looked into her eyes then returned his focus to the gun as he began backing down the stairs. "No, no, no" he whimpered. Never taking his eyes off the gun, he slid into the darkness and disappeared into the street after stumbling on her doorstop. The sounds of his footsteps running away echoed off the buildings of the narrow side street.

Megan walked down the stairs to the bottom one step at a time, then pulled her keys from the outside lock and closed the door without looking into the street. The mix of adrenalin, fear, and power with her alcohol buzz was a strange high. With a new pride in herself, she headed back up the stairs to the kitchen sink, washed her hands to remove the lime from the tequila shots, then dropped the gun into her purse and left the apartment feeling safer and more in control of her life than she had ever enjoyed before.

CHAPTER 5

▼

GUANA BAY, JUNE OF THAT YEAR

With the rising sun starting to show through the slats of the wooden shutters on the bedroom windows earlier that summer, Dana rolled over and snuggled up to her husband's warm body. *This reminds me of winter! We may need to raise the temperature setting on the air conditioner now that I am used to tropical heat,* she thought as she softly ran her hands over Andy's back and rolled him over so that she could kiss his chest and explore between his legs. Feeling him start to respond, she buried her head under the covers. A small smile tugged at the corners of his lips and he sighed, half awake and half asleep as he felt his wife's mouth touch were her hands had been.

After 14 years of marriage and successful careers in the States, Andy and Dana had found themselves in a new chapter of life. Andy's long time business relationship with a needy friend, Nat, had brought them to the island to straighten out another one of his messes. It was starting to sound like a line from one of the old Laurel and Hardy movies. Andy was always helping Nat years ago back in the states and the adventure of living in Paradise quickly reduced any concerns they had of Nat's cavalier and often bizarre approach to personal and business relationships. Unfortunately, Nat's bad behavior had escalated and Andy was constantly dealing with his lies and secretive approach to daily events. Andy had no intention of continuing a business relationship with someone who might even be breaking the law. Nat seemed to be getting very friendly with some unsavory types from the late night bar crowd and to top it all off he was showing too much attention to one of his employees who had a full time and angry boyfriend. An explosive emotional situation was brewing, and it concerned Andy. After many attempts to bring his former friend back to the high road, Andy gave up. Breaking up was hard to do, unfortunately. A court case was underway because of the termination of the business relationship, and it was certain that Nat and Andy would never be friends or business associates again.

The lawsuit was minor compared to a recent evening of terror. What started as a relaxing evening perfect for reading a good book and sipping wine would quickly send shock waves of emotions that threatened to completely upset and reorganize the simple island life the couple had enjoyed since arriving in the Caribbean. Andy was out for a quick business meeting with a friend and Dana was enjoying her newest purchase of a recent New York Times bestseller. Dressed in her signature comfort clothes: a pair of Bikini Beach drawstring shorts and short spaghetti strap top which she always wore braless, she rested comfortably and re-read the cover's promotional information. Well into her 40's, Dana's body had the look that turned men's heads because of her small size and wild curly strawberry hair. Their beach home over looking Guana Bay offered them solitude and privacy. With most houses built far apart and surrounded by lush tropical landscaping, Dana never experienced being crowded by neighbors. Cars rarely even passed close to the house, giving Andy and Dana a sense of isolation. Most days, Dana spent many mornings watering and working in her garden. With a spectacular view of the blue ocean almost everywhere in the house and on the property, they enjoyed countless hours simply watching the palm trees grow, as Andy liked to boast to friends. The truth for Andy was that he liked to watch his pretty wife tinker. Andy never seemed too tired of finding and savoring the beautiful things in his life. Dana loved him for it and teased him repeatedly about having rose colored glasses.

Once, a visiting friend from the States had some fun with the same observation of Andy's demeanor. "You know, if Andy was walking through a farm pasture and stepped in horse shit up to his ankles, he would probably scream with delight *I found the pony, I found the pony.*"

As Dana sipped more wine and studied the first few pages in the novel, her concentration was interrupted by a light knock at the door. *Andy must have left his key in the house.* Within seconds, there was another soft knock. Placing her book next to her glass on the coffee table, she stepped barefooted over the sleeping cat by her chair to cross the large living room past the big open kitchen bar.

Approaching the tall wooden front door, she grabbed the deadbolt key releasing the lock with an audible snap and opened the door. Expecting to see her husband, she froze in surprise. Two men, both wearing jeans and black T-shirts quickly forced their way into the house and closed the door with a slam. Not believing their actions at first, Dana was stunned. She regrouped quickly then examined her intruders carefully. Both men were of dark complexion, wore flip flop sandals, no jewelry, and appeared to be early or mid 20's. The taller one of them raised his right arm to reveal a small revolver and said with a strong Caribbean accent, "Where your man, bitch?" Dana stood silently trying not to scream and watched as the other man rushed down the hall and searched both bedrooms and bathrooms. After opening and closing several closet and bathroom doors, the man returned and continued his search by opening the terrace sliding doors and checking the pool area.

"Nothin', de bitch must be alone" growled the smaller man as he walked back into the living room.

"Where da fuck is he? His car out front" yelled the gunman.

"My husband and a friend left in another car for a business meeting. They will be back at any moment. Listen, no one needs to get too excited or angry. My purse is on the kitchen counter, there's several hundred dollars in it, and my ATM card. Take it. I will even write down the pin number for you so that you can get more cash. The keys to the car are on the table by the door. Take it too. Just leave. No one needs to get hurt, okay?" Dana's army training and self control kept her steady, but she watched the gun as most people do when confronted with a weapon.

"Dis ain't no robbery, Lady. Dis ain't about us leaving wid your cash. Dis is about you and your husband leaving. Da island. Dare's some people who want you gone, and we gonna make sure you get da message" the gunman spit with a lewd sneer and a wave of his arm. Turning to face his friend and stepping closer to Dana, he grabbed her shoulder and pulled one side of her top down revealing most of her breasts. "Hey Whip, dis bitch not what I expected. He say dis older couple was ordinary and the guy 'as some gray hair. But dis little sweet cunt be nice. Look at dem tits. All nice and suntanned. You like to show dem, don't you, ho?"

Dana still had not moved from the entry area and the gunman saw her eyes dart from his gun to the door handle which was only a few feet way. He pushed her aside, turned the deadbolt key, and threw the keys into the living room. Then he moved toward the sofa. The cat bolted from the room and ran down the hall toward the bedrooms. "If we gotta wait for da man, den we might as well be entertained. Tink so, Whip? Can you imagine hubby's surprise when he returns and finds his naked bitch sucking my rod? Come over here and hold her for a sec. I want her to get a good look at what dis man has in his pants" he said putting the gun down on the nearest end table as he rubbed the crotch of his jeans and unzipped the fly.

Dana felt the other man step behind her and push her into the living room. The hot air and sour smell of this breath on her neck moved her forward faster than his hand. He stopped her by grabbing her shoulders then he pulled her top over her head. She was now only a few feet away from the taller man. He reached out and fondled her right breast then dropped his jeans to the floor. He was not wearing underwear and his erection grew as he pulled on himself. "Hey Bitch, bet you never seen someding as big as dis cock before. Huh? I can't get over dem pretty suntanned tits! I might fuck dem first."

Great. I am stuck in the middle of a sick porno movie, and I can't get out. Where in the hell is Andy? He should have been home by now. And the sight of this mean son of a bitch with his pants down around his ankles and his ugly dick in his hand is starting to piss me off.

"Get on your knees for Mr. T-Man you stupid Ho."

Dana obeyed. Sandwiched between the two men, she surveyed her situation. Both men were young, in good shape, and probably getting hornier by the minute if that was possible. She might be able to disable one of them but two? Her chances were slim at best. Once the sex started they would probably be holding her arms too tightly for the movement she needed. *At least they put the damn gun down.*

"Hey T-Man. I get some of dis nice shit too" the man called Whip whispered behind Dana's ear as he also kneeled and reached around her to feel both breasts. Then he pulled on the waist of her shorts and stuck one hand down to feel her ass as he braced her shoulder with the other arm. "Dis be some premium pussy! I bet dis tight ass will beg for more of my dick."

"No worry Whip. If dey don't get off dis island fast, we are gonna come here every week and tie up de old man and fuck dis cunt over and over. Dat will convince dem to get de hell out of here. Or maybe dis hot momma will want to stay with us for more good loving after da old man runs. Maybe we just fuck her at da same time. You take one end, I fuck da other." He stepped forward menacingly with his pants dragging the floor so that her head was level with his erection. As he continued to rub his penis, he pushed his hips back and forth near her face. Both men now chanted, "Yeh, yeh, come on baby" in a sick unison. The man called Whip was drooling on her back as he continued to tug on her shorts but so far he had been unable pull them down over her hips. In the kneeling position Dana had her legs spread slightly for balance as she prayed that her pants would stay up. Neither man heard or saw Andy enter the room from the terrace and grab the lamp on the end table. But Dana did. She dove to her left as soon as she saw Andy raise the lamp. With the scream of an ancient warrior, Andy smashed the lamp sideways across the larger and nearly naked man. The blow from the heavy lamp sent the would be rapist crumpling to the tile floor where he lay limp and bleeding. The other man, Whip, still on his knees, looked up at Andy with complete surprise. Dana jumped forward towards the end table and grabbed the gun as Whip rolled over, then stood and pushed Andy aside. Without looking back at his friend, he ran out the terrace doors. With the gun in hand, Dana jumped up and quickly followed the fleeing man to the edge of the swimming pool deck. Stopping before entering the garden, she fired twice into the darkness then slowly lowered the pistol.

"Shit, I missed." Dana assumed when she did not hear a scream from the man or the thump of a body fall.

Still shaking and breathing heavy, Andy looked at his wife with relief as she stood outside. "Damn, I really liked that lamp."

"Your concern for your nearly raped wife is underwhelming, Andy." came Dana's immediate response as she wandered back to the house. Andy quickly moved to her side and they stood in the sliding door entrance.

Andy continued, "Thank goodness it shattered and didn't bounce off of that bastard's thick skull. Remind me to replace it with another easy to smash version. I'll check eBay in the morning in the home security section!"

"Oh, great. Now my husband is shopping for new furniture."

Andy pulled his still topless wife into his arms. "Thank God you are okay."

"I'm okay. But you need to hear what they told me. I am just damn glad that you started watching Major League Baseball in your old age. You swing a lamp like a home run superstar." As they held on to each other tightly, their tears began to flow.

Dana composed herself first. "How did you know they were in the house?"

"Tom dropped me off outside the gate and drove away. I walked into our parking area to examine the condition of some of the garden accent lights when the silence of the night was broken by their profanity. It didn't sound like a TV sound track so I came around the back to the terrace. I lost it when I realized what was happening. I entered the room in rage before I had a plan of attack. Stupid, but true. The anger I felt seeing you kneeling on that floor in front of a guy with his erection waving in your face robbed me of any reason. The lamp was the first thing I saw, so I used it."

"Hey, it worked. Thank goodness. Did you know that they had a gun?"

"I never saw it. Until you went for it on the table, that is. Creeps like that usually run when the odds are no longer in their favor, so I counted on the fact that one lamp would be enough once it smashed against his head."

Dana studied her husband's eyes. "Listen, you did good, even without a plan. Lucky for him your weapon of choice broke into pieces or you might have beaten him to death."

After a minute or two Andy released Dana from his embrace. "Now let's find some duct tape and decide what to do with our ugly friend in there."

Turning to the scene of the struggle, Dana started laughing softly. On the floor where the bleeding man had been lying was a pair of jeans, two flip flops sticking out of the legs, and glass and pottery from the broken lamp. But no man. *Now the porno movie is turning into a comedy.* **Half naked man seen running from married woman's home** *will probably be the headline in the Daily Herald newspaper tomorrow.* "Honey, this is getting to be too funny."

Andy was not as amused. The man was probably still in the house. Showing serious concern, there was no humor in Andy's face as he put his finger to his lips in the classic "be quiet" mannerism and pointed down the hall. Dana handed Andy the gun and they crept cautiously side by side turning on every light switch they could reach. The horror and fright from earlier was back. The home they had come to love had become a place of terror and the monster they were seeking could be lurking around the next door. Reaching the guest room, Dana reached in and turned on the light. They looked around carefully then quickly relaxed once more. The terrace doors were open and there was blood on the white banister just outside. The small palm plant in a ceramic pot on the other side of the railing had been knocked over. There were bloody foot prints on the white cement tiles leading into the yard. The big bastard without his pants or shoes was gone.

CHAPTER 6

▼

JULY OF THE SAME YEAR

Technically the off season, the summer months bring a steady but smaller flow of visitors to the island Paradise. Many full time workers who push themselves with 6 or 7 day work weeks during the winter months take advantage and enjoy cutting back during the less demanding days of summer. Conrad bounded out of his boss's office on the 2nd floor of the St Rose Arcade over looking Great Bay and jumped two steps at a time down the stairs to the Front Street Entrance. In his excitement he almost ran into three young women walking past the corner clothing store window. Stopping dead in his tracks before knocking one of them down, he smiled sheepishly and allowed them to walk ahead. This was a great day. Not only had his boss praised his work and dedication, but his pay was raised from $8.00 per hour to $12.00 with an additional paid week of vacation per year. Plus the company would begin paying for his yearly work permit renewal. The boss even handed him $800 cash to reimburse him for his last permit. *About time someone noticed my contributions to this damn company.* All three of the women, probably tourists, turned as they passed and made eye contact while looking him over from head to toe. One of them blew him a kiss. *Now that Bitch is hot.* Crossing the street to avoid walking through a group of female barkers soliciting hair braiding, Conrad was greeted by the constant invitations from the cruising taxi drivers, "Back to the ship? Back to the ship?" *Damn, you would think that they would remember me. I walk these streets every fucking day.*

Slowing his pace to blend with the hustle and bustle of the busy shopping day, Conrad paused to visit Hot Dog Man under a shady tree and buy a dollar ice cold beer. It was only 10:30 in the morning, but he was in the mood to celebrate. Plus he had the next three days off as comp time for working late nights and Sundays. Sipping from the bottle, he leaned against the corner of a store while watching the many tourists from the ships and hotels navigate with small maps of the store locations. Several had walkie talkies in hand and squawks of communication from family members echoed on the street. "Where are you now? Where should we meet? Did you find towels?" One couple across the street outside of a jewelry store appeared to be in a heated discussion about a purchase. Several parents passed dragging children who whined and cried about going to the beach. A couple passed in the process of kissing while the woman held out her left hand and showed off a new diamond ring to no one in particular. The amount of tattoos and piercings in full display on men and women that passed Conrad was amazing. Low cut halter tops on women young and old displayed body art on breasts, shoulders and arms. He noticed the groups of two or three shop workers standing to the side of store fronts smoking cigarettes. It seemed every time one group finished, another group took their place. Even though smoking was still allowed in bars and restaurants, no stores allowed food or smoking. Drinks were a different matter. Several of the jewelry stores were quick to offer a cold beer or a glass of champagne to any couple looking at expensive rings or watches.

To Conrad, the throngs of tourists were a necessary evil. At least not all were old and over weight. Two more attractive women in see through beach cover ups approached and both were wearing thong bikinis. *Now there is some classic ass.* Conrad started to greet them but quickly retreated when he noticed two men following in muscle shirts, bathing suits, and matching water taxi wrist bands. This group was traveling together and the men scanned the street with jealousy from side to side as their women strutted their stuff and turned on the alley to the beach. Conrad followed this small parade for one more lecherous gaze after they passed him and ordered a second beer. *Oh shit, maybe next time!*

An older couple paused near the hot dog stand as the man handed over a dollar and pointed at his beer choice. The wife raised her camera and snapped a photo. "Honey, no one at home in Virginia will believe that it is legal to drink out in the street here."

"Baby, no one in Virginia Beach can wear a thong on the beach! Never mind while shopping on the main street of town" was the man's reply as he took in the sights of the passing tourist women.

"Dirty old man."

"You didn't mind last night" laughed the man as he gulped the beer.

"Come stand by this welcome sign for a souvenir photo, okay?" asked the woman.

Conrad watched them without comment as he tossed his empty bottle into the trash can.

"Do you have a moment" the woman asked as she looked directly at Conrad. "We always return home and have photos of each other from vacation but very few together! If you don't mind, could you take a picture of us?"

Conrad stood and replied unenthusiastically, "Sure Lady" as he reached for the camera.

The couple moved together and posed for several shots while Conrad fired away with the digital camera.

"My turn to say thank you and buy a round … have another beer, young man!" was the husband's response.

"Your nickel" replied Conrad as he and the older man clinked bottles in a toast. "Did you come on one of the ships today?"

"No" the wife replied. "We own a time share at a Ski Lodge in West Virginia and traded for a week here just to give it a try. This is only our second day and we are ready to buy a few weeks on this island! What fun! Great beaches, fantastic restaurants, English is spoken every where, and the people are so friendly. We will be back, for sure. How about you? What brings you here?"

With a shrug Conrad paused to gulp this beer. "I guess the question might be what keeps me here. Since I am from the USA, I am not allowed to remain over 90 days as a tourist. I came to visit friends and found a void in my field of expertise: security for retail stores or loss preventative action as we call it. Most locals want jobs in banks or Government offices if they even need to work at all. Retail and related fields are always looking for workers. Construction is worse. And the hard jobs of gardening, maid service, and other low paying positions are always short handed. Plus, not many folks want to work weekends, Holidays, or off hours. The result is opportunity for those who will do what is necessary for business to survive and prosper. So I stay, legally, with a work permit."

"Well, that sounds like a win-win for guys like you who are willing to live on an island." observed the older man.

"Yeh, but the work permit process is never easy and is filled with delays. My last renewal submitted in late 2004 was approved for pick up in July of 2006. When I received it, the date of expiration was September 2006. Crazy stuff." commented Conrad as he took the last swig of beer from the bottle. He caught the eye of Hot Dog Man and ordered more cold beers with a quick wave of two dollars.

"If you guys are going to drink beer all morning, I am headed to Little Switzerland and Coach for a little shopping!" waved the wife.

"You can't drink beer all day, if you don't start in the morning" proclaimed Conrad.

"Okay, Baby. I will find you there in a short while." Turning toward Conrad he extended his hand. "By the way, I am Bob and my wife is Kathy. Glad to meet you, and thanks for the beer."

Conrad was starting to feel a buzz. *What a great way to spend the morning. Finally some fucking praise from the boss. Surprise cash in his pocket. I hope Megan doesn't find this cash. The Bitch will want a new piece of jewelry.* "Good to meet you, Bob. I am Conrad. My girlfriend is Megan. She works just down the street."

"Is she American, too?"

"No, South African. She came here as crew on a Mega Yacht and stayed. But not with a work permit. Her boss is an asshole who tries to cut corners on everything including keeping his employees legal. His employees are constantly disappearing into the tourist crowds when the Immigration police make a sweep down the street. I doubt if the son of a bitch pays taxes either. I wish she would find a different place to work. I don't trust the guy. He is a letch, if you know what I mean. Always slobbering over her." *Sometimes I could just kill that asshole.*

"The price you pay for having a pretty girl friend" replied Bob.

"Well, it fucking pisses me off" snarled Conrad with a fist in the air.

"Alright then" answered Bob as he looked at his watch. "I should try to catch up with my pretty girl friend before someone scoops her up."

"I thought you told me that Kathy is your wife."

Bob looked at Conrad and raised his arms. "She is. But she is also my girl friend." Turning away he handed Hot Dog Man another dollar and announced, "One more for my photographer" as he joined the crowd walking down the street.

"What ever." Conrad accepted the next cold beer and returned to his rest position leaning against the building in the shade. *Damn, I am getting hungry. Time for a sandwich or something.* He surveyed the crowd again and started to move back towards several restaurants when he noticed a blonde walking from an alley with Nat. Immediately he recognized the walk. It was Megan and she was leaning too damn close to that skinny son of a bitch. Conrad pulled back behind a group of window shoppers so that they would not see him as they entered Front Street. Instead of walking towards him, they turned in the opposite direction and moved at a leisurely pace smiling and talking. Conrad dropped his now empty beer bottle in the trash and followed.

"Thanks for inviting me to help pick up the boxes at the airport, Nat" cooed Megan as she touched his arm. "I needed some fresh air and a break from all those tourists today more than anything."

"What's up?"

"Conrad. He is making me crazy. I just don't think I should stay in that apartment with him anymore. I don't love him."

"Then just get your own place and be done with it" answered Nat as they turned toward the parking lot where he kept his car during the day.

"It is too expensive. I know you pay me what you can, but I need a roommate to afford a place by myself. Even now, Conrad and I share expenses on that little place we have and we rarely have money left over to blow."

As they approached his car, Nat produced the keys and opened his own door then flipped the automatic lock for the passenger side. "Well, just keep looking for a roommate and things will eventually work out." From the far alley, Conrad watched them get into the car then he turned and ran the three blocks to Back Street where his car was parked.

I hope the bitch put some gas in here recently. Conrad jumped in and started the engine after a few turns. Quickly turning toward the Salt Pond he spotted Nat's SUV stopped in traffic headed in the direction of the hill. Conrad's old white sedan was a former rental car and looked exactly like most of the cars in traffic. *Fleet automobiles are great when you want to blend in.* Since Nat's large SUV was much taller, Conrad could stalk them without any concerns for being noticed by the couple. He followed them all the way to the airport and saw them turn into the cargo bays that delivered incoming merchandise air shipments. Not slowing as he passed them, Conrad continued to the Maho Hotel area and used the round-a-bout to reverse his direction. There were several cars parked outside of the airport fence so he found a space and waited for them to leave the cargo compound. Within 10 minutes, the SUV appeared and turned back towards Simpson Bay and the hill. Conrad once again melted into traffic and followed. Ahead, he could see the traffic lined up in a stall. *Damn, the fucking bridge is up. Without air conditioning, I have to sit here in the hot sun while that Bitch of mine enjoys his new car and cool AC.* Conrad killed his engine and reached in the back seat to crank down the rear windows. Then he noticed Nat walking through the lines of stopped traffic. *Fuck! I hope that son of a bitch didn't see me.* Conrad slid down slightly as Nat turned toward one of the convenience stores and went inside. The open bridge was clearly visible to traffic for about a half a mile, so several people exited cars and took the opportunity to stretch their legs or buy a cold drink from a nearby store or vendor. Nat reappeared with two bags and jumped back in his car with Megan. Conrad took the opportunity to get out of his vehicle and move closer to the SUV for a better view. Nat and Megan were looking at each other as he fumbled with something in the bag and pulled out a bottle of wine. Conrad watched as they poured drinks into plastic cups and toasted. *I guess you can drink during work when you fuck the boss.*

The bridge started down and people returned to their cars as Nat adjusted all of the air conditioning vents to blow his way. "Damn, it's hot when traffic stops for this fucking bridge. I should have sent your ass into the store for the wine."

Megan pretended that he didn't say that and took another sip. The traffic once again moved forward. "Since you bought two cold bottles, it seems a shame to go straight back to work. They really don't need us today. Want to stop somewhere like your apartment?"

Behind them, Conrad had re-entered and started his car in pursuit.

Nat appeared to consider her request but adjusted the radio volume instead. The traffic on the hill gave them time to listen to two more songs and drink another full glass of wine each. As they passed the Salt Pond downtown, Nat purposely missed the turn for the office parking lot and continued east. "I have a better idea. My housekeeper is at my apartment so I don't want to go there now. We can ride out to one of my favorite spots at Le Galion beach. The breeze should be strong on that side of the island today and we can relax out of sight of everyone who knows us in town. Philippe brought me some good grass last week on his sailboat. Look in the glove box."

Megan's heart soared and she quickly agreed, "Sounds great to me. What ever you want … you're the boss."

As he followed, Conrad was not surprised when the SUV did not return to the parking lot. Traffic started to thin, so he dropped back further by slowing down to intentionally catch the light. He watched them turn left and head east away from the Front Street shopping district. *Where the fuck are you going, Asshole!*

Several delivery trucks backed into traffic in his lane and Conrad was forced to sit longer than he expected. He could see men stepping up to other stopped cars and making conversation with friends. Impatiently, Conrad beeped his horn and let his anger rise. "Today, today Idiots! Let's get moving! Fuck!" he screamed inside the car to no one in particular and without success. The car's radio in front of him was so loud that the bass thumping not only drowned out Conrad's ravings but shook his car. He grinned as he remembered reading a joke about Barbara Walters years ago who was asked if she believed in Capital Punishment. *Only for people who play loud music on the streets* was the tag line that he often chuckled over. With the new huge sound systems in the small cars on this island, Conrad found the humor to be more appropriate today.

When the road ahead of him finally cleared, he drove toward the now unseen SUV's direction. *Fuck me. I'm screwed. I totally lost them.* Knowing that he could never find them if they turned off any of the many beach access roads, he stopped by the first neighborhood grocery for some cold beers then drove straight toward Nat's apartment. This side of the island near Oyster Pond had more steep hills than town and one stretch of road had an angle to it that required four wheel drive on a slick rainy day just to get up it. His old rental car had seen better days and the engine groaned in protest as he floored the accelerator to pass the hurdle. *One of these days I gotta get a new car with 4 wheel drive for these fucking mountains. Shit. Engine don't fail me now.* With success, he continued on the hill and parked past the building out of sight on the side of the road. *I think I know where you took her, Asswipe.* Sitting in the car, he gulped down two beers quickly to quench his thirst. Throwing the bottles in the back seat, he opened a third and got out of the car. Luckily there were few houses nearby and he could walk unnoticed. First, he stopped to pee in the bushes. *I would like to be pissing on your grave you worthless prick.* Then he crept slowly down the slight incline to the front of Nat's building. Suddenly, a small van with rental advertising came flying towards him up the same incline that challenged his car. Conrad stepped back into the surrounding brush, but the driver and a woman in the front seat had already seen him. They slowed and the window on her side came down electrically. He waved his beer and approached them.

Inside, Conrad could see three couples taking up the three rows of seating. Everyone was packed in tightly since the mini van was not large or made for much cargo. A female voice asked, "Does this road go all the way to the top? We want to take a few photos of this magnificent view."

"Yes, but it gets a bit hazardous up there with the narrow road and steep inclines. You need to be careful." answered Conrad as he tried to peer down the front of her loose fitting tank top. The red head was attractive and well endowed.

"It's okay. My husband owns a large earthmoving and trucking company and has experience driving everything you can imagine. We'll be safe. We're on a cruise ship visiting today only and our friends in the back with us wanted to sight see before we return to the ship" responded the sexy redhead with a soft Southern accent.

One of the male voices boomed from the far back seat, "Hell you say! The women wanted to see the view from the top of this mountain. We men were perfectly happy to spend the rest of the day enjoying the views of naked tits at Orient Beach." Laughter followed.

Conrad agreed. "You have my vote on that beach too. I hate driving on these fucking hills, pardon my French, Ladies." More laughter. "But again, don't expect to find safety rails up there. And drive as slow as you can."

Everyone in the van yelled, "Thank you!" as it sped away and up the hill.

Conrad watched in amazement as the driver took the next bend too fast and screeched his tires. *I don't remember seeing those idiots wearing any seatbelts. Are they fucking nuts? Would he drive like that at home? Tourists. Everyone's brain cuts off when on vacation, I guess.*

With the street once again quiet, Conrad turned his attention to the house. He could see the windows and front door of the apartment as he approached but nothing was open. Somewhat disappointed, he cautiously circled to the side and tried to get a peek at the parking pad without getting too close. *Fuck, empty. No one home. Not even a sign of neighbors. Three families live in the building and not a sign of anyone.* He took another sip of the beer he was carrying and walked closer just to be sure.

Feeling defeated once he confirmed that the building was vacant, he stormed back up the hill to return to his car. In frustration he threw the now empty bottle into the brush. He heard the bottle break on a rock which was immediately followed by another loud series of crunches from the weeds and trees above. *What the fuck?* He looked up and was shocked to see a side door from a vehicle flying down the hill. It smashed into the pavement 50 feet in front of him as more noise followed. He heard bushes and small trees breaking and the roar of an engine. Suddenly on the ledge above, the same van with the tourists he had talked to just a few minutes ago slammed into a tree sideways. *Holy shit.* More debris fell in front of him and it seemed to rain dirt and twigs. He could hear screaming and crying. Conrad broke into a run and followed the road up to the crash site around the bend. Just above the van, he saw a lady sanding on her terrace viewing the wreck with a cordless phone in her hand. The mini-van was a mess. It had evidently rolled sideways down the hill breaking apart when it hit rocks and hard pavement. Two of the doors had been torn off as it flipped and all of the glass was shattered or missing. Conrad stopped in his tracks when he saw the blood on some of the passengers faces as they lay limply in their seats. He looked up again and saw the woman on the telephone gesturing wildly to someone she had called. *The police have been called. I need to get the fuck out of here. No need to explain to any bastard why I was in the neighborhood.*

He returned to his car, found another beer that was only slightly cold, and headed down the hill. As he turned on the main road to return to town, two police cars and one ambulance screamed passed him in the opposite direction and made the turn to go up the hill. *That was close.* Traffic was minimal heading back into town at the end of the afternoon, so Conrad enjoyed the breeze that was flowing through the car while driving 30 mph. Directly ahead a car backed out of a blind driveway causing Conrad to slow and wait. *Come on asshole ... let's get going. I ain't got all day!* Ahead a single female driver jockeyed her car into position once she exited the drive and proceeded in front of Conrad at a slow pace. Just ahead another vehicle took advantage of her slow speed to cut in front of her as it came out of one of the beach access unpaved roads. The woman braked and honked but the white SUV driver just flipped her off with his right hand and continued in front of her. *Son of a bitch! It's Nat. I found them. Wait. Something is wrong. There is only one head in the jeep. What the hell?*

The woman in the car in front of Conrad slowed and pulled off the road leaving an open space between the SUV and Conrad's car. Nat seemed focused as he drove and only looked forward, so Conrad shortened the distance between them. Suddenly Megan's head and shoulders appeared as she raised herself from Nat's lap.

Conrad could not believe what he had just seen. Megan was inches from Nat. She was smiling. She rubbed his shoulder as he drove. *Sucking on that asshole's dick, for sure.* Rage filled Conrad's eyes with tears and he took his foot off of the accelerator. He looked down at his hands and they were shaking uncontrollably. As the car slowed and he pulled off the side of the road, he began beating the dash board with his fists. "I'll kill you, you bastard! I'll kill you both" he screamed.

CHAPTER 7

▼

GUANA BAY, JUNE

The morning after the attack in their home, Andy and Dana sat quietly on the terrace facing their visitor with coffee and fresh fruit on the table that separated them. Neither Andy nor Dana touched anything or made an attempt to pretend to be hungry, and soon the silence between them was excruciating. It can be amazing how a few minutes of silence in a social situation makes everyone feel awkward. With very little sleep from the night before, both were showing signs of fatigue and stress. Andy had called his friend, Jack Donnelly, before 8 am and asked that he come over to help them sort out the details of the events and to help them decide their next steps. Since Jack was a retired Detective with close contacts in the Philipsburg Police Department, Andy and Dana decided to call him before involving the police.

Everyone was dressed comfortably and casually. Jack wore the traditional shorts and polo shirt that quickly labeled him as a tourist by the locals and Andy had on his at usual home swimsuit outfit, a pair of H20 trunks with a KaKao T-shirt from the French beach restaurant. Dana, a frequent online shopper, wore one of her plunging neckline Victoria Secret's cotton tops with a pair of cargo pants that hugged her butt in all of the places that delighted her husband. The weather was spectacular and the view of the water in the Bay from the terrace was postcard perfect. But the tension in the air reminded Jack of a bad storm coming.

The two outside fans on the terrace softly clicked as they turned overhead and palm trees around the swimming pool moved with the passing trade winds. To a casual observer, the two men and one woman would appear to be vacationers enjoying another perfect Caribbean day before heading to one of the 37 pristine beaches. Finally Dana broke the stillness. "Some coffee, guys?" she asked as she leaned forward to pick up her cup from the teak table. Without drinking any, Dana set the cup back down.

Jack had a momentary thought as he watched Dana's breasts during the forward movement; *damn my friend is a lucky man. And I am a pathetic dog for lusting after his wife. What did President Carter say once about lusting? It sure got his butt in trouble fast.*

"No. I had two cups at home before Andy called so I am slowing down on the caffeine rush with this one" replied Jack. "Besides, beer is my favorite breakfast food" he joked in an effort to relax the couple. Andy feigned a smile and sipped a glass of water but turned sullen. This was not going to be a relaxing morning. Jack knew that victims of any crime ride a roller coaster of emotions full of anger and relief if they were lucky enough to escape bodily harm. Despite the Rambo type rescue that Andy had pulled off and Dana's quick recovery of the weapon, worry and feelings of helplessness were bound to linger and haunt the next few weeks. It always looks so easy in the movies. But real people have real emotions and complex reactions to danger. Because of his experience, Jack was extremely patient. He sat without comment as Dana covered every detail she could remember of her time with the two intruders before Andy arrived with his magic lamp trick, and then listened carefully as both Andy and Dana told of the escape of the two men. Even the lightly comical description that Dana gave of the half naked man probably running down the street knowing that the wild woman behind him in the house would not hesitate to fire the gun and shoot him in the back, did not bring smiles to either of the couple. Jack could feel their emotions ebb and fall as they purged themselves of the fear, anger, and disbelief of the horror of the situation they had endured the night before.

"Well, Jack. What is your take on this?" asked Andy. "Because the more I think about this the more I would rather not involve the police. We have cleaned the blood and the mess from the broken lamp. Even though we have the jeans and sandals in a bag, we could have found them anywhere. Neither Dana nor I have a mark on us. And not even one of the neighbors lives close enough to even react to the two shots that Dana fired at the first guy when he ran. Producing an illegal weapon may make us look suspicious or worse yet suppose the gun is traced to a recent crime? Then we are really screwed."

Jack shook his head in agreement and placed his coffee cup on the table. "First, it is interesting that they refused Dana's money and did not strike her. It would seem that their purpose was purely psychological. They were probably told not to leave injuries or marks on either of you. Fear of sexual assault and humiliation alone would give a lot of people reason to flee. Add to that the terror of having a loaded gun pointed at you during a home invasion. We expect to be safe in our home. The street is different. Dark parking garages are different. But our home? Our home is the ultimate refuge. And physical pain could be saved for the next visit if this one did not work. They expected an older woman in the house so it is obvious that they had never seen Dana before. Someone sent them specifically to terrorize you and chase you off the island. This is clear. They knew what Andy's car looked like, expected both of you to be home ... perhaps finishing dinner and some wine in a relaxed and vulnerable state of mind. They came early in the evening so that you would answer the door without hesitation, and expected to control the situation with the gun. What is interesting is the tall man's statement that some people want you off the island, but later he only refers to one person. But then again, we are not dealing with rocket scientists here. We can't hang our conclusions on every word they spoke to Dana. These two guys can be hired for a job like this for a few hundred bucks each, and they are dumb enough to think that they can escape into the night and never be found. Who knows if one person hired them or two? Bottom line is that we have eliminated robbery as the motivation. Now, let's talk about your law suit with your former business associate and whether or not you are in more danger. I assume that you still have the revolver?"

Dana sat up straight and looked Jack directly in the eyes. "You can count on that."

Jack just shrugged his shoulders and said, "Dana, get a dog. I don't recommend that you keep an illegal gun in your home. Now, I doubt that the sexual attack was planned or anticipated by the men. Once they saw Dana, it was probably just a reaction to her attractiveness so they were taking the opportunity."

Dana blushed. "Were they stupid enough to think that my husband would return, find me raped or beaten and buy tickets for us to return to the USA without hunting them down first? They called each other by names, for goodness sakes. They did not wear masks. Or do you think that they would have killed us or me after the attack?"

Jack looked at them and reached for some fruit. After placing a few pieces of apple and pear on a plate, he gestured with his silver fork. "I knew a couple in the restaurant business here a year ago that were tied up and threatened with a hand gun. They were told to leave. Rumor was that they upset a competitor by taking away some major banquet business. In the days before the attack, they were warned to back off, but they only laughed at the attempt to stop competition. So goons were sent to make the point clear. One visit was all it took to scare the pure shit out of them. They booked tickets back to North Carolina and were gone in less than a week. Stories like that get around. Of course, they had two small children so the motivations were different, I guess."

Dana agreed with a shake of her head. "Nothing could be more terrifying when the safety of children comes into the equation."

Andy interrupted them. "Jack, there is only one son of a bitch on this island that would want us to leave. Nat. Our business and personal relationships are over. We are suing him for well over $250,000 plus attorney fees and court costs. Plus we know many details of his cheating the Island Government of tax dollars, hiring illegal workers, and taking large amounts of cash off the island without any declaration. If you ask me, it is amazing that he did not send some thugs to threaten us long before the law suit was filed. If he didn't send those guys to shake us up and drive us away, then I must be missing something. It is too obvious."

"Okay, I admit you have a likely suspect. But without involving the authorities, how do you expect to tag him to the attack?" Jack looked directly at Andy and then back to Dana. "You do want to stop him don't you?"

"Damn right I do. I want to kill the worthless piece of shit" snarled Andy as he stood, smashed his glass of water against the terrace's side stone wall and stormed off down the hill past the swimming pool leaving Dana and Jack speechless.

CHAPTER 8

▼

LE GALION BEACH,
WEDNESDAY, AUGUST 20

Tourists visit the island of St. Maarten to enjoy pristine beaches, fabulous gourmet restaurants, duty free shopping, and an environment that offers relaxation from the stress of everyday life at home. "We're not in Kansas, Toto" to borrow the words from Judy Garland. Thirty seven beaches, gambling, and all night bars and clubs add to the excitement of the vacation experience. For the serious historians or interested visitors, two forts have guarded the harbors from the 1700's and museums document the early Arawak Indian inhabitants as well as the struggles between the European countries for domination of the Caribbean. As the world changed and transportation improved, many cultures made the Caribbean home and battles were fought over land control. However, since 1648 two Nations, one French and one Dutch, have shared the island in peace. American tourists come in record numbers. But on this calm and quiet morning, Jack Donnelly found himself following the request of his friend in the Philipsburg Police Department by driving quickly to the beach where a dead body was found that morning. Arriving just after 8 AM, Jack had driven a bit too fast on the unpaved road. With the dust flying around his jeep he spotted a crowd ahead near a clearing of trees. After parking beside two French police vans, he approached the group of police, medical personnel, and emergency vehicles near the beach, and moved towards the officers in uniform gathered near a parked car with all doors open. As he had done this many times before when it was his job in New York, he quickly adjusted from a relaxed retiree to an observant Detective. Walking in the sand to the vehicle, Jack could see many foot prints and tire tracks. *Too many people on the scene already. This won't help with clues.* He noticed immediately that there were no smiles and few greetings of "Good Morning." *No one likes to see Paradise interrupted.* Only serious faces turned to look him over.

Le Galion Beach, situated on the East side of the island and accessible only by the long single dirt road, was clearly French territory so Jack was not surprised to see the area surrounded by French Gendarmes as well as the Dutch side Police. This was their jurisdiction and they were in charge. However, the Dutch license plates on the car in which the body was found offered the Gendarmes the opportunity to quickly involve the other side's police both as a courtesy and to facilitate the early stages of the investigation. With little residential or commercial development close by, the beach attracts many locals for wind surfing, picnics, and horse back riding during the day. At night, the isolation provides an ideal spot for outdoor sex, under age drinking and once every few years, murder. Too often abused by users, the area is not pristine and does not remind anyone of a resort postcard scene. Tire tracks, used condoms, beer bottles, and paper trash litter the sand close to the foliage. With that ignored, the darkness and privacy is exactly what nocturnal visitors seek.

The island enjoys a reputation of friendliness in that violent crime, rape and murder are rare. Perhaps the legal houses of pleasure keep the testosterone under control. Perhaps the warm weather and soft breezes relax the aggressiveness of plain old fashion evil people. Who knows? The violent crimes usually are domestic in nature involving the passions of lovers, neighbors, and family. The vacation visitors are almost never a target of crime except for the usual cameras and shopping bags carelessly left in open view in rental cars. So Jack understood the Lt. Governor's sense of urgency in obtaining facts on this murder quickly.

As he walked closer to the late model SUV Jack could see a male body sprawled across the back seat. Fully dressed in jeans and a white shirt with boat shoes, the body laid slightly slumped to the side revealing a pony tail on a Caucasian male who appeared to be in his mid or late 40's. Men with gloves walked around the vehicle while a police photographer shot several pictures. Standing off to the side were a few members of the press, also snapping photos for the front page of the next day's newspapers. No one leaned into or on the car. Jack acknowledged several police men and women, but remained passive while they secured the scene of the crime.

As footsteps approached, Jack turned and caught the eyes of a familiar face, "Good Morning, J.R., what do we have here?"

J.R. Holiday was obviously taking charge of the investigation despite being on French soil. The serious nature of the scene showed immediately on the face of the St. Maarten Investigator. "Dead male. His age is probably in the 40's. Pony tail but mainly used to comb over a thinning head of hair. Slight build. No identification. No visible tattoos. We ran a check on the car since I called you earlier this morning and it belongs to a business on Front Street. We have called the business phone and the owner's emergency cell number from police records, but there are no answers at either number. We assume the owner must be the dead man in the car. Everything in the car is gone. No insurance papers, title copies, or inspection information. Clean, with all paperwork removed just like from the victim. No cash on him and even the keys are missing from the ignition. He was shot through the head at close range with what appears to be a small caliber weapon judging from the small hole and absence of much blood. No struggle. We found what was left of a joint in the ash tray by the seat. There were lots of cigarette butts, beer bottles and used condoms on the ground but it is hard to tell how long they have been there. No discarded weapon found yet. Someone took the time to clean out the normal personal items inside the car but missed a small bag of grass and some packs of condoms in the glove box. It also appears that his left ear was pierced and we are told by some of the officers here that the owner of the business that owns the car was known to wear a large diamond stud, but there is no earring that we could find. No watch either, but he has a tan line for one. Optimistically, we do not have an attack on a tourist. With 6 completely local murders in 8 months, we still have safe tourism. Thank goodness. This may have been a robbery, and this guy probably knew his assailant. Or he may have pissed someone off royally. Many emotional dramas are known to be played out in this lover's lane. The robbery and clean up could have been staged to hide the actual murder motive. He could have been caught with his pants down while doing the dirty deed with some guy's wife. You never know. Just a few years ago two women tried to kill a younger girl who was sleeping with one of the women's boyfriends. Sex and murder seem to dance together at times on this hidden piece of Paradise."

Jack touched his own chin in thought, "Okay, but his pants are up. And money and murder are married quite often too. At least he had time to relax and finish what ever he came here to do ... except for the bullet that exploded in his brain everything looks peaceful. On first glance you might think that he is simply sleeping off too much rum in the back seat. Who found him?"

"The story of most early morning body discoveries ... a jogger." replied Holiday.

"No chance of suicide on this one, that is for sure. Good work on the background. You move fast my friend." Jack commented.

"Thanks, but this is not a fancy or clever police investigation show on television. This is real life stuff. We don't have a team of forensic scientists combing the scene for evidence. We have to base the investigation on what people tell us, unfortunately. Most of the Gendarmes speak very little English, so they are leaving that up to us. French side or Dutch side, we all want to protect our tourism industry from this type of tragedy."

"How can you be sure this is not a random crime? Certainly a guy with a business on Front Street in the Tourist section could be transporting lots of money after a busy cruise ship day. This guy could have flashed some cash around the wrong person without even knowing how stupid that can be."

J.R. pondered the thought for a moment. "Possible.... but crazy to walk from a store to go out drinking while carrying lots of cash. Don't you think? We assume that we are not dealing with a tourist on a first time holiday to the Caribbean who drank too much rum. If this is the store owner tied to the auto, this man lived here and operated a business. That would not make sense. Also, if the buzz we are hearing checks out, rumor has it that this guy was screwing a bunch of people on the island in several ways. So cleaning his clock might have been inevitable, if you ask me. Right now we don't have a positive ID, so everything is pure speculation until the French send the body to Guadalupe for autopsy and we get a friend or family member in to look at the body."

Jack paused, looked back at the body again inside the SUV and turned with a question. A few flies started to buzz around the head wound. "What kind of information has to check out?" *It won't take long for this auto to start to sink to high heaven.*

"Here is a stoke of luck ... one of my police officers on the scene today told me that a week or so ago he overheard a late night drinking conversation in one of the bars of a brothel in which one of the local well know bad boys was mouthing off about getting even with some guy on Front Street. It seems this businessman contracted for an American couple to be shaken and stirred to chase them off the island in fear. But the attack failed. The henchmen were overpowered by the targets and chased off. It seems some Front Street businessman was irate and refused to pay the balance of the money for the attack as agreed. My officer did not get much in the way of details, but he heard that the guy paying for the attack was slender and drove a newer model Ford Explorer. My officer knows that the big guy who did the talking at the brothel is mean and rumor has it that he is often armed. This bad boy was pissed and wanted the rest of his money for the job. Just a few minutes ago, my man put two and two together when he arrived and saw the car and body. It could be connected."

Jack only looked at J.R. and wondered *Are whorehouse stories like fishing stories?*

"Any way to ID the guys in the bar who made the threat?" asked Jack.

"If we can, but you know how that goes. We will have to dig around and try to find someone who gives us an accurate description of the men. My officer did not get very close to them that night. He was trying to hear the whole conversation without being noticed. Then again, he was off duty and in the bar to drink and relax."

"Well, good luck on that one. I feel your pain."

J.R. Holiday turned and raised his voice to the Dutch side police under his command, "Six of you sweep the area for a weapon! And bag everything you find."

Putting his head down J.R. added quietly so that only Jack could hear, "At least this littered beach area will be clean of beer bottles and other trash when we leave today. But I bet that my men will kick sand over the used condoms."

In a more normal tone he continued, "Then there is another lead. The French Gendarmes reported that there is an all night sex club in the lowlands that experienced a disturbance late last night which involved what was believed to be a local Dutch side resident and not a tourist. It seems that they only allow male/female couples. Two men and two women arrived and started to drink heavily. Both men wore jeans and white shirts. The women with them appeared to be window dressing. There was quite a show for attention. It seems that there was lots of rude language and macho displays of sexual aggression toward the women walking past. A few times they pissed off other male guests of the Club. The guy matching this description had to be asked to leave when things got spicier than they allow. He and a French speaking male friend quickly upset many of other visitors. The two men did not leave quietly. They abandoned the women they brought with them to the club and several threats were yelled back and forth between the bouncers and the ejected men in the parking lot. Then it appeared that as they left the two men started arguing among themselves too. One witness told the Gendarmes that she thought that she saw a gun being waved about inside the front seat of the SUV as they were driving out of the parking lot."

"Everyone remembers seeing a gun after a body is found." interrupted Jack. "They just become foggy on the details."

Waving his hand in the air with a gesture of agreement, J.R. continued. "No clear description of the SUV but everyone was sure that it had local tags, not rental plates. The two women left behind turned out to be paid escorts who had never met the men before. They told the Gendarmes that they each received $200 for hanging out with the guys and partying. They insisted that sex was not negotiated in the agreement. Strange. The Gendarmes were quick to tell us that the girls looked very hot and available."

"Shit, is that the private club with open group sex and cameras in every room? What could be too spicy for that group?" asked Jack feeling like an over the hill kind of a guy.

The Inspector only smiled knowingly, "The idea is make love, not war. These guys were too angry and too loud to make the other visitors comfortable. So the Club was quick to remove them. We are trying to get a copy of the parking lot surveillance tape, but needless to say the Club is very private about the activities there. They don't want us to see any famous visitors or heads of Government on film."

Jack rubbed his chin in thought. "Well, I see. I guess. Any chance we could interview the women?"

J.R. Holiday broke out laughing and looked directly into his friends eyes. "Jack, the two young Gendarmes over by the Land Rover gave the ladies a ride home from the Club ... and they say that they forgot to get their names. Sorry."

Jack sighed, "And that is their story ... and I am sticking to it."

CHAPTER 9

▼

PHILIPSBURG, WEDNESDAY
MORNING, AUGUST 20

Beep, Beep, Beep, Beep

"Damn it Megan! Shut that thing off!" Conrad was yelling from the other side of the bed. The alarm was getting louder with each successive reminder and Megan could not move or reach it. *If I move my body my head will explode.* She cautiously tried to separate her cracked and dried lips to respond to him, but the words could not come out. Irritated at the continuous buzzing sound from the alarm and Megan's failure to move, Conrad threw back the light weight comforter and rolled over her to shut off the alarm clock. The rocking bed of an old worn out mattress and the unwanted weight of Conrad's flabby stomach on her back was all that it took. Megan could not stop her body's urge to purge. She hung off the bed and grabbed the trash can. As she threw up the countless Tequila shots that had gone down so easily a few hours before, her emotions were running out of control like a pack of wild horses. Conrad sat up in disgust. *Why did I go back into the bar after Nat left? Drinking those shots was a mistake. They just made me angrier. The whole night made me a crazy person. All the places that I went. Conrad is bound to find out. Oh shit.*

"You fucking slut. Whoring around on me again and drinking to unconsciousness on a Tuesday night ain't enough when you know we have to work in the morning? You got to stink up my bedroom too? When did you get home? I fell asleep and it was way after 2 AM, you slut. Was it that asshole boss of yours? Is that where you where? And where the hell is our car? I didn't see it outside."

Sure Conrad. You passed out drunk when you came home and never even called my cell phone. Immediately, Megan thought about Nat. The disappointment of last night. The blood rushing to her head as she watched Nat and his friend. Those two assholes at the restaurant and her having to run away from them. Her confused feelings. Her anger. Coming home in the wee hours and slipping next to Conrad without waking him. While the room continued to spin, Megan held on to the trash can and tried to settle her nausea and shaking. She started to answer him, but could only produce a weak moan. Then she felt the bed shift as he got up and reached for his pants on the nearby chair. She knew what was coming. His belt made a swishing sound as he pulled it from the waist band and popped it on the sheet next to her. Then he pulled up her long T-shirt night cover and started to whip her naked buttocks slowly, waiting and watching the skin redden between each strike. Releasing the trash can and burying her head in her pillow, she let the tears flow.

∗   ∗   ∗   ∗

Megan had grown up in South Africa in an affluent middle class family. Her parents had provided a loving and comfortable home for her, her older and talented sportsman brother and brainy younger sister. Being the middle and average child, Megan was never outstanding at anything. Then puberty hit and with her big blue eyes, long blond hair and developing centerfold figure, she adjusted her ambitions to making her way in the world without the talent of sports or the accomplishments of higher education that were so evident in her siblings. To her parents chagrin, after high school she began waitressing in a restaurant frequented by Yacht and Chartering owners, guests, and crews. Money, alcohol, drugs, and beautiful sun tanned skin mixed with the excitement of far away places reached by boat in the ultimate luxury of the rich and famous. It was not long that the chef of one of the largest Yachts, a young and handsome French man, started paying extra attention to her and remaining at the bar until the end of her shift. After a few passionate visits to his cabin on the "Voyager" one of the largest and most luxurious charters to travel the Mediterranean and Caribbean, Megan was ready to accept Herve's offer to join his restaurant staff and share his bed every night. She was in love.

During the next four years, Megan and Herve shared long busy days with guests aboard, brief stretches of privacy and relaxation when the yacht was not in use and the passion of their nights together. Their good looks combined with his French accent and her English accent made them favorites for the paying guests and delighted the owner when he was aboard. Even though the money was not great, living expenses were covered in the lifestyle, and Megan began to save money for the first time in her life. Each port brought new experiences, new charter guests, and her ability to judge lifestyle options grew. While they were docked in St. Maarten for the first time due to the opening of a marina designed for the larger boats, Herve excitedly planned to take Megan on a complete tour of the island. He had lived briefly on the island while in High School because he had taken a summer off to visit his Grandparents in their Orient Bay Villa. Herve was sure that Megan would love the night life of the island, the pristine beaches, the numerous casinos, and a chance to finally eat at a different restaurant every night. And love it she did. When the yacht made its summer trip back to Europe, Megan told a heartbroken Herve that she needed time apart. Too many drunk guests (sometimes both female as well as male) grabbing her ass as she cleared the dinner table, too many 10 and 14 day workweeks with no time off, and too small a crew cabin convinced the 24 year old woman that it was time to find a job on dry land. Perhaps she would write a book someday. It could happen. She would finally compete with her successful brother and sister in the eyes of her mother and dad after all.

*   *   *   *

After another pop of the belt, Megan lay still and waited for the ordeal to be over. Conrad pushed a pillow under her stomach as he raised her pelvis and spread her legs apart. She heard the squirt of the KY tube and felt his fingers enter her ass. As his knees rocked the mattress he grunted with pleasure as he moved his penis into position and grabbed her hips. Anal penetration was a big turn on for Conrad, so she knew he would not last long. Seconds later she felt his warm semen splash across her back as he whispered, "You're my little whore. You're my little whore. Don't you forget it."

Thank goodness he did not want to pull the gun trick again.

Megan remained motionless and listened to the sound of the shower. She wasn't 24 years old anymore. She was 31, living on an island and in a relationship with a man who beat her and forced her into loveless sex. She considered the defeat and the admission. She was sharing her life with someone who beat her and she had allowed it. Carefully carried out, always her fault, and never leaving a mark that was not covered by clothing. Why was she staying? How could she allow this? At least the son of a bitch never hit her face. He would punch her stomach, he would whip her, and he would slap the back of her head. But he would not leave evidence that could keep her from working or arouse suspicion among friends or co-workers. At one time long ago, everyone in their social circle thought that they were the golden couple. Always ready to party. Always at the right function or grand opening. Now there was constant conflict. Arguments so frequent that conflicts became routine. Yet, most of the times the sex was more exciting with a fight. It was hard for her to explain to herself.

Megan's head was still pounding from the emotions of last night. It was a damn mystery how she possibly could have driven home that late given her mental state. Thank goodness Conrad walked to work because of the limited parking in town, so she had plenty of time to clean out the car before he found any thing. As the water was shut off, she heard him finishing in the bathroom with the sound of an electric tooth brush and the hum of the hair dryer. Nervous and jumpy, she tried to slow her breathing and lay as quiet as possible when he entered the bedroom and opened the closet doors. She could sense him watching her as he dressed but she made no attempt to cover herself or begin to start her day. Putting on his shoes, he sat down next to her and gently caressed the small of her back. "You know I love you baby," he whispered as he moved his hands up and down her thighs and between her legs. Moving his hands to the side of her face and then pulling firmly at her hair he added, "I know you're awake Megan. You don't fool me for a fucking minute. We can continue this discussion later. Now get up and get your sweet wet ass ready for work. And clean up this mess."

CHAPTER 10

▼

PHILIPSBURG, WEDNESDAY EVENING, AUGUST 20

Overlooking the Great Bay harbor in Philipsburg there exists the remains of a Dutch fort built in the 1700's to protect the entrance to the city from invading armies by sea. Fort Amsterdam has unfortunately been ignored by governmental funds to protect and preserve this valuable tourist attraction and link to St. Maarten's past. With the surrounding land owned by a resort, at least the site does not attract garbage. Crumbling and without enough historical markers to explain the meaning of the remaining ruins, it sits quietly with few visitors to disrupt its peace. Because of the elevation, it affords a terrific view of the water to the east and west. As the sun slowly lowered in the sky and changed the sky to warm yellow and orange colors, Megan sat on the wall of the old fort and poured another glass of white wine into a plastic cup.

The day had been filled with turmoil. She arrived late at work because of the scene at home with Conrad this morning to find the store's front door sealed by a large lock from the tax inspector's office. Looking through the windows, it was obvious to her that the police had already searched the building. A police car remained parked out front, inside the building all of the lights were on and the place was a mess. Rumors ran rampant on Front Street all day. Everyone knew that the body found at Le Galion Beach was certainly Nat's since the car had already been identified by the license plate. No one had seen Nat all day, and police were also searching his apartment. Everyone had a story to tell. There were those who speculated drug or money laundering activities. Others threw out intriguing anecdotes of Nat's getting in with the wrong crowd and upsetting powerful people with his abusive behavior. Many looked at Megan and asked where her boyfriend was last night. No one seemed to believe that the murder was random or without passion. Police were moving up and down the street asking more questions. Even the store's landlord, well known for his hot temper and violent outbursts, was questioned for almost one hour. Conrad was surprisingly cool to Megan when she stopped by his office to see him. His lack of concern or interest in the murder made her uncomfortable but she asked no questions of him. After this morning's episode, she needed to keep him calm.

Just last night at the Greenhouse she was filled with the hope of a new love. She saw dreams of a new life and new power. Today, she mourned loss. Immediately, she was without a job. Even if the store reopened, it would be months or even over a year. Who knows if Nat even had a will? The selfish bastard probably thought that he would out live and out smart everyone. His business could be thrown into legal battles and confusion. Already the tax guys were at the door. What next? Her earned wages due at the end of this month would never be paid. Officially she did not exist. Nat had paid in cash and off the books to avoid the taxes and Labor Department obligations. She was now totally dependent on Conrad. With the high season coming to an end, jobs in town would be hard to find and obtaining a work permit for a new employer might take even more months. Life was turning as sour as the trash can she puked in this morning before Conrad beat her and forced himself on her.

One thing became clear this day. She had to find an alternative to her lifestyle. Full time waitressing or bartending was the obvious solution. With her blonde hair, a pair of very short shorts and a skimpy top, tips would be good and several of the bars in Simpson Bay were in need of help after the last Labor Department raid. Many workers without permits had been arrested and deported. The bar owners were desperate for help. She could take one of the small bus rides over the hill every evening and hope for a ride home later. Buying a car was not an option at this point. But Conrad would be furious and her only alternative would be to move out of his apartment. Starting without the necessary funds would make the change very difficult. She had some cash hidden, but not enough. However, the risk might be worth it. She could meet a wealthy mega yacht owner or newly divorced executive here to gamble and chase ass on the beaches. It could happen. It had happened. Timing was everything. The wine was giving her a feeling of new promise. She poured more and listened to the familiar splash of the liquid hitting the plastic.

She sighed, held her wine cup up in a toast toward the setting sun and said, "Fuck you Nat. You let me down. May your sorry ass rot in hell."

CHAPTER 11

▼

A FRENCH SIDE BEACH, FRIDAY, AUGUST 22

Just after 9 PM on Friday night after the murder, T-Man waited at the water's edge in a Go Fast boat as Whip brought another car load of Chinese men and women to the edge of the beach in the French Lowlands. The Chinese had arrived in St. Maarten earlier that day by air through St Eustatius with the help of a well paid "friend" at the airport Immigration office. No one in the group spoke a word of English, so a local Chinese businessman rode with Whip on each trip to pick up more riders from a safe house several miles away. T-man hated the wait and possible exposure to either the Gendarmes on land or the Coast Guard at sea. *Why don't they just bring all of them in a fucking bus?* All running lights on the boat were off and the big man would not even allow himself to light a cigarette until he was far off shore and on the way with his shipment to St. Thomas. He watched as the Chinese sat absolutely silent under a tree between the road and the shoreline. Slowly the group grew in size and T-man's pulse quicken with the thought of his large cash payment for this ride. He could cover the approximately 100 miles to St. Thomas in less than three hours if the seas cooperated and be back to visit a local whore house before it closed in the wee hours of the morning.

T-man did not consider him self a cruel human trafficker preying on the poor or the weak. There was plenty of bad stuff out there. He knew of young pretty girls brought in by promises of good jobs or waiting rich husbands only to find that they were forced into labor or sexual servitude. Tonight the Chinese on his boat were paying lots of money to migrate to lands of opportunity. When Nat first approached him and offered the financial backing, T-man almost told his mother to assure her that he was not in the drug business like in the past. He would be helping people. He was noble for sure. Now, after many night runs he swelled with more confidence than ever. He wondered if he needed Nat anymore. *Hell, I provide all of the places to hide dis boat.* It might be time to open his own business! It would be nice to keep all the money and perhaps run a delivery from time to time with some of those pretty women who come voluntarily to whore houses. He heard stories of the girls from Thailand and the Ukraine. *Dat would be worth a reduced fee!*

After taking another careful look up and down the beach, T-man opened the only bottle of water on the boat and sipped it slowly. A bag of chips from earlier was now empty so the next few hours would be without food or water. He needed to cram as many of the immigrants on the boat as possible with plenty of fuel, so space was a premium. The Chinese passengers were allowed a soft fabric back pack or sack, but no luggage or other items. He hoped that they had followed instructions from their countryman and not eaten or drunk many liquids. The trees by the beach were their last chance to pee and he hated when a passenger became sea sick. Although his boat had a VHF radio it would be off. Only the compass at the helm would be used for this trip. T-man checked his hunting knife on his belt and the small handgun hidden under his shirt in the small of his back. He borrowed this gun from a friend after losing his to that crazy bitch over in Guana Bay. If he hadn't been so focused on her tits and getting his dick sucked, he might have heard the damn husband enter and been able to shoot the motherfucker before he smashed the lamp over his head. You need to be on guard. No doubt about it. No problems yet with passengers, but he heard of captains that had to throw illegals overboard when they freaked out during long trips. Rough weather, broken engines, and human fear could set off some asshole without warning. T-man wanted to be ready if the situation required it or it some slimy goon deserved it. Besides, when he borrowed the gun for tonight from his friend they talked about what an ass wipe Nat had become. His friend promised to help recover the money Nat refused to pay after the home attack went bad … one way or another. *My friend is one crazy and mean mother, too. Speaking of crazy motherfuckers, I wonder where Nat has been all week. Usually he is crawling up my ass when we make a delivery run. Greedy as hell and he does nothin'.*

Whip's car returned for a final drop. T-man watched as the local businessman directed the entire group to the waters edge and explained in Chinese that they could wade into the water and board the boat. Without a comment, every one of the immigrants raised their bags and moved carefully into the calm surf. T-man pulled the first man aboard then moved back to the bow to prepare for the trip. Quickly the men and women helped each other crowd into the hull of the boat and pack together without talking. In the darkness he could see Whip accepting a bag of money from the businessman. Whip used a flashlight to count the bills then accompanied the man to his car which was hidden in the trees. As soon as the car disappeared down the road, Whip walked to the water's edge, flashed his light briefly and waved goodbye. *Man, this be much better than the drug business. No guns fire when the money switch hands. No grabbin' the stuff and running.* T-man grinned and waved back to the shore as he pulled up the anchor line.

Without any seating in the Go Fast boat, the passengers crammed themselves on the floor boards hoping to find some comfort. One young woman reached under her butt and brushed her now wet jeans to shake off the sea water that sloshed from side to side in the bottom of the boat. T-man heard her saying something in Chinese that sounded like protest to the man next to her.

"Hey Bitch! Dis ain't the Queen Mary" the big captain barked as he placed his hand on the handle of the hunting knife. The passengers stayed silent and the young woman hugged her partner without looking up again. *No one likes wet feet or a wet butt.*

T-Man started one of the two four stroke outboard engines once the anchor was aboard and left it in idle as he pointed the bow toward the open sea. With the motor in gear, the boat moved quietly but slowly. After a few minutes, the lights from vacation villas in the Lowlands started to fill the horizon behind him he increased speed and started the second engine. The boat quickly reached a plane over the water and cut through the waves without navigation lights. The big captain considered a smoke, but decided to wait. After about 15 minutes from shore, he suddenly was aware of a larger ship moving quickly over his right shoulder in pursuit. Hoping that the ship was a pleasure boat, he pushed the throttles forward to maximum and continued to look behind.

"Shit. Where in da fuck did dey come from?"

Suddenly the sound of a marine hailer from behind broke through over the sound of his engines. With a firm voice came a command, "To the vessel without lights … this is the Coast Guard. Stop your engines and wait for us to come along side. Repeat. Stop your engines immediately. This is the Coast Guard."

The panicked passengers suddenly erupted into nervous chatter and wails of fright. One man tried to stand and move forward over his fellow travelers, but stumbled from the wave action and fell backwards as T-man screamed, "Down, sit down you fuckers!" He waved his left arm pointing down as he held the wheel with the other. *They can't catch and board me at this speed. And they sure as hell won't follow me for 100 miles. I just need to keep on getting on …*

"Vessel without lights … this is the Coast Guard. Stop immediately. We will fire if you refuse to stop."

Shit, it may be dark but they can see me. They should see the passengers. They won't fire at me. I ain't running no drugs. "Fuck you Assholes!" he screamed.

The previously calm waters were developing larger swells causing the boat to rise and fall more dramatically with the speed. The Chinese passengers now yelled with each pounding of the bow. T-man held his speed and continued to turn his head forward and back nervously wishing that he had not drunk the water just before shoving off.

As he looked down at his frightened passengers he balled his fist and yelled, "Shut da fuck up!"

"Vessel without lights … you have 30 seconds to stop your engines or we will fire."

T-Man suddenly thought of his real name. Theodore. He hated the name but his mother believed that it sounded presidential for some crazy reason. She never talked about his father when he was growing up on Dominica, but he figured that the old man must have been a real bad dude. He hoped that his father would have been proud. Since he was always bigger than the other boys his age, taking control was easy. No one fucked with him except older boys and he quickly learned to beat them too. When he left school after 7 and half years of worthless education, his mother became distant and resigned to the angry attitude of her adolescent son. Coming to St. Maarten 11 years ago was a needed break from the guilt of dealing with a mother who seemed to love and forgive him no matter what trouble he got into. Christmas when he called her, she asked if he had a job. He lied and told her that he was changing oil for cars at a fancy Dealership. It seemed to satisfy her. She knew he liked cars and could fix them. After this run, he might go to see her. Show her that he was something now and not some drug runner. He thought for a moment about Whip's real name: Waldo. *Maybe these pussy names just made us bad asses.* Then he chuckled. Nothing could stop him now. The open sea would offer safety as he put more distance between his boat and the Coast Guard vessel. Pushing the throttles up once again just to make sure he had maximum speed, he enjoyed the roaring sounds of the big outboard engines and the thrill of the chase. He could hear more warnings and orders to halt from behind but he considered them meaningless. Standing tall and occasionally glancing down at his terrified passengers, T-man let out a roar of joy and defiance at the very moment a large caliber bullet fired as a warning shot from the Coast Guard boat smashed through his skull and sent a large section of his head flying into the darkness of the water.

CHAPTER 12

▼

PHILIPSBURG, SATURDAY, AUGUST 23

Saturday morning after the murder, Jack drove slowly down Front Street in Philipsburg, the shopping Mecca, admiring the palm trees, quaint old world styled pavers, and scantily clad female tourists walking from store to store. *Thank goodness these women ignore the tour guides who promote dressing up when shopping. Wearing a bathing suit just makes you feel better. That's what vacations are about. Duh. You enjoy the things you don't do at home.* Jack also noticed the dutiful husbands that followed close by carrying the brightly colored bags from the jewelry, electronics and perfume stores or travel boxes of duty free liquor. Several men sauntered with a bottle of ice cold beer in one hand, sipping and smiling as they enjoyed an obvious freedom that they could not find at home. *Is this a great country, or what?*

Only a few years before her death, he and his wife Catherine had taken a cruise that included St. Thomas and St. Maarten. Catherine joked with him that she wanted to take another honeymoon every year that followed. Anyone of the couples on the street could have been Jack and Catherine. He sighed and wanted to hear those familiar words, "Do I look fat in this?"

Luck was with Jack today. As he turned into the Pasanggrahan Hotel parking lot at the front entrance to this historic property, he quickly slipped into an empty spot in the shade perfect for his small Suzuki jeep. Palm trees and tropical plants transformed the parking area into a soft transition from the retail store fronts on either side of the hotel. One of his Indian friends, Chandra, smiled and waved hello from the doorway of his jewelry shop. At the hotel Oli, one of the owners, looked up and waved from the side porch as she relaxed with a cup of coffee and the morning newspaper. Caribbean porches are made for sitting. This one was excellent for people watching too since it faced the busy tourist shopping corridor. Jack waved back and continued into the historic building and out to the restaurant veranda on Great Bay Beach. Built as a home, the hotel had a long history of housing dignitaries and royalty before becoming a guest house after the turn of the century. There is even a "Queen's Room" since the property was often occupied by the Royal family as legend has it. Janet, Jack's favorite bartender in town, was preparing the beach bar for today's visitors and the sand was full of sun seekers who were anxious to shed the pale complexion of home for the warm glow of a St. Maarten tan. Jack found a seat at a table for two and arranged the salt and pepper shakers absentmindedly. Feeling a presence, he looked up and was handed a cold Carib beer with a slice of lime protruding from the bottle.

"Good Afternoon Jack, nice to see you back in town" snapped Janet with a slight air of sarcasm. Janet obviously liked to see regular customers more than once per week.

"Thank you. How is your world?" replied Jack as he gripped the ice cold beer and pushed the lime into the top of the bottle.

"More busy at this restaurant and bar since da murder. Lots of police and tax investigators in da store since Nat's body found. Somehow dey all find a way to end up here for a late lunch or an end of de day drink after spending hours in de office and warehouse. I don't know what dey found, but dey sure return a lot to look for more. Yesterday we had some Immigration officials here and guess what? De were met by American big wigs in de banking business. Lots of Suits, and Chinese embassy folks. It hard to figure out what goin' on, but it don't look good. Suddenly everyone showing much interest in what Nat was up to. I even heard bangin' in there like someone is tearing out walls or shelves lookin' for stuff."

"Just think Janet. You might end up on CNN!" teased Jack.

"No, no, no. I ain't talking to no camera about no murdered man. No. It be bad luck. Very bad."

As Janet moved quickly away to another table to greet some diners, Jack leaned back and watched several families walk by. Old and young, everyone gazed about and strolled along the walkway without urgency. Children wearing tennis shoes seemed to be skating on the back of the shoes. Jack shook his head in amazement. A young couple strolled by with IPods in their hands and wearing headphones. They held hands with their free hands. Never talking to each other, both man and woman seemed to be perfectly entertained.

What could be a better sound than the water lapping on the shore? What is with the headphones to block out nature's sounds? I must be missing something. Jack wondered. He took another sip of the cold beer. A small white cat slinked up to the table and lay down by Jack's feet. Several geckos scurried by on the terrace banister keeping a safe distance from the cat. The soft breeze from the water and the 86 degree temperature comforted Jack's soul and reminded him that he was in the right place. The sadness of missing his dead wife, Catherine, suddenly was heavy on his heart. He stood up, walked closer to the boardwalk, and then turned back to the table. The cat watched him carefully but never moved. Then he was snapped back to the present when J.R. Holiday entered the terrace and approached him with broad smile and his hand in the air.

"Hello Jack. Sorry I'm late. You know how heavy traffic can be on an island with only two stop lights! We have to be patient. I hope you were not preparing to leave?"

"Not at all, my friend … I saw a young couple walk by and had a sudden attack of lost love. I have no idea why I was standing up."

J.R. extended his hand; grabbed Jack's and held it instead of shaking it. Both men paused, released hands and sat down at the table. Neither was embarrassed.

Janet was quick to reappear with two menus, two glasses of ice water, and a frozen Guavaberry drink for the Police Inspector. Without a word, she disappeared again before the men could speak. Jack looked down at the cat still lying by his feet, and then he studied the menu that he knew so well.

"I have many pieces of the puzzle to run by you this afternoon, Jack. Hopefully you can take a long lunch. It is official, so enjoy. My expense account pays for this one! There are many new developments that make this murder more complicated than we originally thought."

Jack felt a surge of interest charging his brain with the joy of returning to the hunt.

"First, let's start with his rental apartment." explained J.R. as he took the first sip from his frozen drink. "We found over $600,000 in cash stuffed in office file folders, various drawers, in between T-shirts, and above the kitchen cabinets. We also found small quantities of marijuana, some Viagra and lots of condoms. Keep in mind that the guy rented the place so most of the household items were not his. Usual bachelor stuff that the landlord says Nat owned: nice flat screen TV, surround sound system, home computer, etc. Kind of odd, but we did not find a single item belonging to a woman. Yet he was known to be quite flirtatious and verbally aggressive on a sexual basis with women, almost obnoxious at times and rumor had it that he was often seen with other men's girlfriends or wives. Then you have the cash. His business showed a very small profit tax last year and it lost money the three years prior. We are having the tax inspector study his gross receipts, cash register records, and stock purchases for the store over 3 years, but nothing adds up to a profit of $600,000 to be taken home and left around the house. Hell, he did not have a safe. Even I have a safe at home for my wife's jewelry and I don't have much cash!"

"The thock pickens. I suppose." answered Jack.

"Huh, I never get your New York humor." replied J.R. somewhat confused by Jack's play on words.

"The Plot … never mind. My poor attempt to make light of a more complicated situation. Police squad room humor. Always an attempt to lighten the mood. A habit we have for dealing with some pretty grim situations and I guess I haven't gotten over the habit yet. The vic must have had additional sources of income and was slow to find a laundry for the cash."

As Janet returned to take orders for lunch, both men returned their attention to the boardwalk, the beach, and the joy of people watching. Jack decided to have a tuna sandwich on French bread with crispy fries and J.R. took the fresh catch of the day blackened with a salad.

"Tini probably caught that fish early this morning, J.R." speculated Jack.

"That is the great thing about a restaurant owner who loves to fish. Every day is fresh fish day! And he and Oli even eat here most days. When the owners are the most seen diners, the food has to be wonderful." agreed J.R. as he finished his frozen drink and switched to the water on the table. "While the office on Front Street did not have a large amount of cash, we did find some interesting paperwork."

"How so?"

"Well, we found a receipt from a St. Thomas boat dealer for a Go Fast boat, purchased 4 months ago and delivered there. Oddly, there was no name on the receipt, just cash. Someone was not worried about getting warranty work. The boat is expensive and yet there is no record of a registration to Nat in St Thomas or St Martin. No one we interviewed so far even mentioned that he own a boat."

"Suspicious for sure. Why buy an expensive toy and then hide it?"

"He probably did not want to be tied to the ownership or the use of the boat. Hiding a boat in plain sight is easy when you have the numerous coves, lagoons and inlets that we have. But I will get back to that boat later. It turns out that his full name was Norbert Allison Turner, not Nathan as most people assumed. Never married as far as we can tell and no siblings or other living relatives. Since he had large shredders in his office and at home, we don't know much about his life back in the states yet. This guy liked being private. We did not find anyone who knew his real name, but his nick name seems obvious. And certainly not unusual these days to use a name other than the birth name around the island. A lot of Expats like to keep some parts of their identity anonymous. What we could find in paper records did not indicate any large inheritance or source of money to substantiate the cash we found. His business was ordinary in a resort community. T-shirts, hats, sunglasses, topless bathing beauty postcards, press on tattoos and the usual tourist novelty items one would expect to sell in town. We sent his home computer and lap top to Police Headquarters in Curacao for examination but everything was password protected and I don't expect much in the way of results. His Palm software was not protected so we reviewed his calendar and address book. Odd, there were no business meetings listed. Also odd was that he collected lots of personal information on people."

"Like what?"

"Well, besides details of phone numbers, fax, email, mailing addresses and the usual he tracked birthdays, wedding anniversaries, even some social security numbers if the person was a USA citizen, and he even listed spouses and pets names. Strange for a man to do that. Hell, my daughter has to call me to remind me of my wife's birthday and our wedding anniversary! Plus we wondered how he got some of the very intimate and private information. You are even listed. He must have met you at a bar or restaurant and asked you personal questions as he was getting to know you. You know what I mean … conversations with fellow American citizens or other Expats, friendly and relaxed. People talk a lot after a few rounds of drinks in those beach bar environments. Just getting to know ya! Then afterwards, he recorded the answers in his palm address book. Weird, in my opinion. You can't help but wonder what he planned to do with such detailed information or why he spent so much energy on it."

"Damn. I didn't realize I was that good looking or interesting."

"Trust me, Jack. You are not."

Jack laughed. "Sounds like the guy was an armchair detective or voyeur of some type."

"Or he liked to have things to get over on people, if needed. Blackmailers are often power junkies." added J.R.

"Ah, yes, the little man syndrome. Did you find a steady squeeze to interview?"

"No, just the rumors of him chasing anything wearing a skirt. Especially the ones who already had boyfriends or husbands" replied Holiday.

"Well, it is safer that way. They can't just move in on you after the first date." Holiday nodded his head in agreement.

The food arrived and Janet refreshed the drinks. Both men started eating and thought about the strange complexity and contradictions of the dead man's life uncovered so far by the investigation of his apartment and store office. The cat at Jack's feet stood to stretch and smell the tuna, then retuned to a sleeping position at his feet.

As they both enjoyed the food silently for several moments, Jack was the first to speak. "Since I have not seen a lot of water skiing in our local waters and no racing clubs have been formed that I know of, do I assume the boat was purchased for drug running? Let's think, large amounts of cash, a fast boat, Caribbean waters, murder, and the summary seems easy to figure out."

"Hardly." answered J.R. as he poured more of the restaurant's homemade dressing on his salad. "The guy was American. Drug smuggling is best left to the South American experts. However, there is a popular and less dangerous way to smuggle today."

"And what would that be, if I may ask as a retired police guy left out of the flow of information?"

"People, my friend Jack. People. Chinese people, Haitian people, Dominican People ... let's think about this for a moment. Your name is Connelly, correct? I bet that your ancestors were not Native American. For what ever reason, they arrived in New York because they wanted a better life. What did they pay to get there? What did they find? Were they accepted by the ruling class? Were doors of opportunity opened for them? I doubt any were opened, Jack. Or did your family arrive in America on the Mayflower? Were they part of the landed gentry?"

"I see said the blind man." Jack shook his head in agreement and thought about the history of his family. Poor immigrants. Immigrants who would work any job to make a dollar. He never asked his Grandfather about the price of passage or the details. Now he experienced a wave of regret for not following family history more carefully.

"Things haven't changed over the past 100 years, Jack. Where ever people are without hope and opportunity, they look to migration. But governments hardly offer or encourage easy legal measures for movement. So migration demand falls into the hands of entrepreneurial folks who provide the means for travel. For a price, naturally. Is it a victimless crime? Some would have you believe that. However, when you mix in the use of corruption or collusion among law enforcement and immigration officials, the need for secrecy, and the need for a network for transit points often the aliens become victims to the system. Inhumane treatment and conditions are common. For profit, boats or trucks are overloaded with people and dangerous conditions spell disaster time and time again. Control is maintained over the human cargo with beatings, rapes, and murder. Stories abound in the Caribbean of traffickers throwing overboard men, women or children when extreme coercion is needed to establish rule. Not to mention the sex industry … where brutality is as common as thunderstorms. Young women are promised legitimate jobs but arrive to find themselves prisoners in whore houses."

"Money is made coming and going." commented Jack dryly.

If Holiday understood the play on words, he ignored it. "Exactly, my friend. Add to this equation the spin off businesses that supply additional support. Travel agencies, bus companies, air lines, marine supplies, and the list expands. Let's not forget the employers who need the immigrants for labor. Labor that often is undesirable to the local population or with low wages and no benefits."

"The French side of this island has a required 35 hour work week." Jack added. "But I see construction sites with men working 7 days a week to finish the job."

J.R. continued, "Listen to the language spoken by the construction workers … I bet you won't hear any English or French! Or find many work permits. Our new airport construction was another great example."

Jack nodded in agreement and started to reply but was cut off by the Inspector.

"Jack, something else came up we need to discuss. The American was being sued by former business partners. Also American. A friendship gone bad. Yesterday I learned that you know a couple named Andy and Dana Parkerson. It turns out that they are the ones who had the relationship with him and who are suing him. Typically on this island, one law suit is matched by another. So this guy was in turn suing them. Lots of angry words have been exchanged according to the attorneys involved. Don't forget that there is a rumor that thugs went to the couple's house to chase the couple away. My information is that Nat may have sent those men to frighten them and drive them off the island. Given the story the officer heard in the brothel, the list is growing for people who wanted to kill this guy."

"Yes, J.R. it is true. My friends Andy and Dana were attacked. Andy was mad as hell. He suspected this guy, Nat. But that does not make him a murderer."

"Mr. Retired Detective, you are quick to assume that his wife is passive. She could have killed him" speculated J.R. as he finished the last piece of the delicious fish. "We checked her out and found that she has a US Army record and she was an expert shooter. The husband has no military record and no training in fire-arms that we could find."

Jack waved at Janet to bring him another cold beer. There were many things to consider on this beautiful day. Jack debated in his mind telling J.R. about the gun Andy and Dana kept after the attack. He remembered that it was a small cal-iber revolver, but did not remember any other details. Luckily, J.R. changed the focus.

"Another aspect bothers me ... the bad guys in the brothel threatening to attack some businessman on Front Street to collect money. Most of these men don't hesitate to come after money that is owned. They must have had another relationship with this guy Nat. More money may have been promised to them for other work. Why wouldn't they just go to his house and kick his ass? There was plenty of money there as we discovered. Who knows?" J.R. took another look at his lunch plate and moved it to the side of the table. "I love eating here. Just don't tell my wife."

"But if they killed him, why not toss his house? After all, no one found the body until the sunrise." Jack asked.

"My point exactly ... things are not adding up for a robbery. This sounds more like a revenge or domestic type of killing. Passion. Jealousy. Hatred. A love triangle."

"Why not add being in the wrong place at the wrong time or seeing something that no one wants seen? J.R., I feel like we are rambling a bit here. Any more ideas or speculations around the island to add to this mix of possible motives?" Jack added as he played with the label on his beer bottle.

"Jack, I am not Colombo. And we are not organized like a television show that finds the murdered in a one hour segment. Like I said before, let's get real. You are in the Caribbean on an island with limited resources for this type of thing. New York City can afford more in the way of forensic research and technicians. We just ask questions and try to put a puzzle together. Keeping our tourists safe is the goal."

"What happened to the Go Fast boat on the sales receipt you found?" Jack asked.

"I am on it. That was making me wonder too" replied J.R. as he turned to motion for the check. "If the boat is in St. Martin we need to find it and see if there are any tales to be told. We found no pictures or friends that had ever been asked to go for a ride. There were no insurance documents in his files. Nothing. I may have picked up a lead on my way here today, however."

Jack sat up to listen and wondered what could be next in the rumor mill and how many more times the finger of guilt would be pointed at Andy and Dana. Clearly they had a strong motive to kill this guy. Holiday was rejecting robbery as a motive.

"We have a report from the Coast Guard that an attempt was made to stop a boat last night. Boats racing away from shore without any running lights always get the attention of law enforcement patrols when seen but they can be hard to spot. This was just one that was found by accident. When the Captain of the Go Fast ignored commands to heave to for boarding, a chase ensued. Then everything went to hell in a hand basket. The Coast Guard boat fired a warning shot over the Go Fast bow but the choppy seas caused the shot to hit the fleeing Captain in the head. Quite a mess, I understand."

"Ouch." Jack responded thinking about the large caliber weapons installed on the Coast Guard ships. "What did they find on the boat?"

"Besides the headless and bloody body of the Captain? A large number of terrified Chinese immigrants sitting in splattered guts and cold sea water. Men and women. All carrying over night bags, and not one who could speak English Can you imagine cramming all of those poor people on a 20 ft open boat? Crazy if you ask me. Hell, I would not even get on a boat that small with only 3 people! No life jackets. No water supply. The radio and lights were turned off. This boat was probably headed to St Thomas or St John. No identification on the Captain or on the boat. This vessel was definitely not used for day cruises or fishing."

"There are plenty of boats behind houses and in the lagoon. Most are of little notice. Just look at the harbor here. We have not been suspicious of these vessels just within our view."

"No kidding. That boat probably had more lives than a cat. Or at least plenty of different registration numbers. Remember the revolving license tags on James Bond's sports car? That scene gave plenty of bad guys an idea. It was probably hidden in plain sight. They only needed to change to numbers every now and then" Holiday paused. "As for many lives, we found American ID cards of various types in the possession of the Chinese on the boat. Probably all were fake, but at least it indicates that this was an organized delivery to US territory. I remember reading a statement back in the mid 90's by the Director of the CIA that speculated over 100,000 Chinese are smuggled into America every year."

"That is a lot of boat rides, Inspector." Jack reflected.

"That, my friend is a lot of money" added Holiday.

"And dat be a lot of wet feet." laughed Janet as she hurried past with another table's order.

"Bartenders and waiters! Always listening to private conversations!" roared Holiday.

Janet sent the men the international wave and brush off with the flash of her arm.

"Speaking of money, J.R., the ID cards may not be fake in the sense of forgery. They may, however, not be legitimate. One of my Mortgage Banker friends in the US took a loan application from a Chinese business woman who had two different US issued passports with two different but similar names! She even had two social security tax ID's. All documents were real. She just obtained them falsely. Think of the folks who have more than one driver's license active in different states. It happens. People just work the system."

J.R. laughed. "Yes and some folks forget to get a divorce before they marry another person in a different state or country! Seriously, though, I emailed the boat dealer and asked that they send me a stock photo of this Go Fast model they sell. We may be able to match the boat from last night with the cash receipt."

"Good thinking, Inspector. How about the dead Captain? Any way to identify him from evidence left behind at the scene?"

"No, and without a head we are at a loss for a personal identification. One thing for sure, he made sure his pockets were empty for this trip. Nothing in his jeans except a little over $300 in cash, some cigarettes, and a lighter. Plus a hunting knife and a hand gun in his waist band. 9mm automatic. No serial number. It had been filed off. No missing person reports, naturally. And no one called to report a stolen gun."

"Finger prints or DNA?" asked Jack unable to stop himself.

"My friend, as I explained to you in the past. This is not New York City. We have lots of DNA and his finger prints. It is doubtful, however, that his prints are on file unless he has a record in the States or served in a job that tracked employees with fingerprint records. And I doubt that this Captain ever attended any Maritime Schools or bothered to get a license. You can bet that the others involved locally in the human smuggling will not be coming forward to claim the remains."

"Sounds like a dead end."

"Not really. We do have the boat. I just need to wait for St. Thomas to answer me and see if we can tie this trip to Nat's murder. Perhaps he was killed for the boat."

"Ahhh, a clue Shaggy, a clue." added Jack.

"Jack, your American police humor once again escapes me."

J.R. handed Janet a charge card as she passed by and he stood to leave. As he walked casually to sign the check at the register, he turned again to face his seated friend. "I scheduled meetings with his former employees over the next few days. At least the two that I identified and that I could find after calling a dozen or so likely cell phone numbers in his address book. Most were part time, being paid in cash and did not have work permits. They tend to disappear whenever the police come knocking. By the way, Jack. I like your cat. She never takes her eyes off of you. Are you going to take her home?"

Suddenly feeling some guilt from his recent all night escapades with Cheryl and Susan, Jack looked up sheepishly at his friend. "Do I look like I need companionship?"

CHAPTER 13

▼

GUANA BAY, AUGUST 29

Can time heal all wounds? Andy was doubtful. Although the days passed after the home invasion and the murder of Nat, Andy and Dana were slow to return emotionally to happier times. They started going outside the house again for fun and making love more regularly but they avoided discussions about the attack, Nat, or Andy's temper tantrum in front of Jack Donnelly. Both were experiencing a sense of relief that gave them some assurance that Whip and T-man would never visit again. But something remained unsolved. *Security. What is the next shoe to drop?* Andy often thought to himself. *I wonder what shit comes next. Do we have false hope?*

One night earlier that week, while enjoying pizza outdoors in an Orient Bay café, Dana spotted a ragged dog lying in the sand near the roadway. "Whose dog is that?" she asked the owner of the restaurant while Andy paid the bill preparing to leave.

"Don't know. He just appeared a few days ago." answered the restaurant owner.

"Is he okay? Does he have water and food? Is anyone looking for him?"

With a quick motion, the restaurant owner picked up the dog and walked to Dana and Andy's car. "Open the hatch. All of your questions have just been answered."

One thousand dollars in animal hospital charges later, the now beautiful and healthy pure bread Coconut Retriever guarded the terrace at their home and never left Dana's side as she moved from room to room.

While watching the new dog patrol the terrace before sitting at her feet, Dana saw her husband outside enjoying his ritual pool cleaning. The sun was especially strong this morning. Andy took additional precautions by wearing a shirt and cargo shorts to provide more coverage from the strong UV rays as he worked. "Hey Andy, I guess I don't need to keep that gun anymore with this beast on the lookout."

Seeing Dana standing by the door topless, Andy admired his wife from the pool and responded, "No you don't. I got rid of it anyway. Jack warned us about keeping an illegal gun around."

"When did you do that? Where is it now?"

"Don't ask."

"Andy, I'm your wife. A gun was used to threaten us. I recovered it and my prints are all over it. I deserve to know where the hell it is now."

"Not to worry. I wiped it clean and put it in a zip lock bag. That gun was probably more than hot. It probably has a history. A 22 caliber gun is the choice of many assassins. Surhan used one on Bobby Kennedy as I remember. I read somewhere that even the Navy seals use them. We did not need to have the damn gun in our home. Besides, Nat is dead. Those guys he sent are not coming back. End of story." Andy turned his back and continued to move the cleaning net around the perimeter of the pool.

Sensing an argument quickly surfacing, Dana turned and reentered the home as she decided to postpone the discussion. This secrecy by Andy over the gun was strange and unexpected for her. Andy just wasn't the same yet. She dismissed her concern just as her dog suddenly turned toward the front door and growled as the sound of a car in the driveway became apparent. Then the dog began barking loudly. Dana hurried into the bedroom to find a bikini top just as a loud knock on the door echoed in the living room. Peering out of the front bedroom window, Dana saw not one but two police cars. Three officers stood near the cars and watched the house as they listened to the sound of a big dog barking inside. The knocked was repeated as Dana returned to the living area. Pausing briefly, she fastened her bathing suit top and looked into the mirror in the foyer. Coby moved between her and the doorway and continued to bark. Holding her dog by the collar, she opened the door and immediately recognized Investigator Holiday. With all of the press that followed the discovery of Nat's body, Holiday was identified in the newspapers as the man in charge of finding the killer.

"Good afternoon. Is your husband at home?" asked the calm police investigator.

"Is there a problem?"

"As you probably know from reading the newspaper, a former business associate of your husband is dead. Shot in the head. Since your husband has a pending law suit against the dead man we need to ask a few questions. Strictly routine. I am sure you understand. Can I see him now, please?"

Dana stared at the Investigator for a moment and considered her options. Seeing no alternative to cooperation, she shrugged and said, "Of course. Let me get him for you."

She paused at the utility room entrance and pushed the dog in and closed the door. As she crossed the terrace and approached the pool, she could see the pool cleaning net and pole lying on the tile. Andy was no where in sight. Confused, she spun around and looked back at the house then out across the yard. "Andy" she cried out, "Police are here to ask about Nat! Where are you?" She noticed Holiday walking toward the pool and looking around as she had.

The only sound either of them heard was the constant flush of the water from the pool pump circulating.

Holiday made no indication that he would leave, so Dana retuned to the house and pulled a pair of white beach shorts and a T-shirt over her bikini. After an hour of polite but meaningless conversation, the Police Investigator left with two of the officers and stationed one man with a car sitting in the driveway. With some frustration, Dana could only explain that her husband would be back any moment. But inside she felt suspicion and anger. *Andy, what in the hell do you think you are doing? They just want to talk to you, damn it.* She peered out the front window occasionally and watched the last remaining officer patiently wait. Then another car, a Suzuki pulled into the drive and Jack got out. After exchanging pleasantries with the uniformed officer, he approached the door as Dana swung it open and pulled him inside.

"Jack, thank god you are here. Andy disappeared when the police arrived and I am so fucking mad at him I could strangle him. What could he possibly think he can achieve by avoiding them and not answering a few questions?"

Jack stood still looking somewhat guilty and gazed from side to side as if hoping to see Andy walk out of the landscaping.

"What is wrong with me, I am so rude. Would you like a beer, Jack? We have Carib and Bud Light. Let's go out on the terrace by the pool. I need some wine." She turned and walked toward the outside bar. Opening the refrigerator she lifted a bottle of French Chardonnay and poured a full glass as Jack leaned on the edge of the tiled counter top.

"Make mine a Carib with lime, please. We need to talk. I didn't happen to drop by this afternoon. Andy called me on his cell only a few minutes ago."

"He did what? What in the hell is going on? Andy calls you and not his wife?

"Andy told me that he was outside on the side of the house when the dog started barking. Instead of walking back to the pool, he peered over the privacy fence and saw two police cars. Hiding behind the big fichus plants he listened to the officers in the parking lot discuss the planned arrest of Nat's murderer. Today. They were certain that the killing was the result of two businessmen fighting over money and the straw that broke the camel's back was the attack on you in your home. It pushed your husband over the edge. Andy told me that he was in no mood to talk to police until he could find me."

"Jack, how did they know about the attack on us? We only told you. No one knows. No one. I need some honest answers before I throw you out the fucking door."

"Okay. Okay. I know. But you are wrong about only three people knowing of the attack. There were also two men who attacked you, whoever sent them, and God knows how many people have heard of the episode during drunken' bar room discussions. You think these people are discreet? Hell, no. I would bet that at least one exotic dancer has heard how bravely these assholes faced death at the hands of some crazy American woman with a gun."

Dana considered his point of view.

"You first should know that the investigator, Holiday, is my friend. We often shoot the shit over a couple of beers and he calls from time to time for advice. I was invited to the scene when they found the body. I have listened to different possible scenarios and offered suggestions. Holiday heard about the attack on you and Andy from a policeman who works directly for him. It seems the guy was at a whore house and heard two known bad dudes drunk at the bar discussing it. They did not name Nat but were angry that the man ordering the attack refused to pay the full freight once the episode was unsuccessful. Your lawsuit, on the other hand, is a matter of simply checking with the courts and giving the dead man's name. It pointed directly to you guys. Yes, I confirmed with Holiday that you were attacked. But since the two thugs must not have told anyone about leaving a gun behind, I said nothing to the police either. And I certainly would never mention Andy's threat to kill Nat that morning during breakfast. He was upset and angry. Lots of people say things they don't mean."

"Yes, and lots of people do things they never say."

"Touché, Dana. However, we can remove the possibility of guilt quickly by turning over the gun and proving that it was not the one that killed Nat."

"Impossible. Andy told me he got rid of it. Remember, it was your suggestion to get a dog and NOT keep the gun." Dana's voice was strained and too loud for polite conversation. She grabbed her wine and took another sip.

Jack thought for a moment and grabbed his beer. "Okay, you have a good point. If the gun was here it would be illegal to possess without a permit so you and Jack could be arrested anyway. Plus the weapon could have a history and any link to other shootings could be another problem. We are in a foreign country. The rules of law work somewhat differently. They can take Andy in for questioning and keep him for a long time. That is why he disappeared. Within a week or so the police may go after his cell phone records and see that he called me today. But they won't see a call to you, so you can continue to claim that you don't know where he is. It could give us time to examine some possible solutions."

"Like what? Running away? Then the dead son-of-a-bitch wins."

"No, let's consider if we have any knowledge to help Holiday. We know that this guy T-Man and his accomplice had a motive. We know that the bad guys had access to weapons. We know that Nat had lots of money and jewelry worth stealing. We know that he was chasing other men's women. What else do we know?"

"That he was an asshole and a totally fucked up individual." replied Dana.

CHAPTER 14

▼

ORIENT BEACH RESORT, LABOR DAY

Even though the island celebrates few American Holidays, everyone is always aware of the impact of them. Labor Day in September often brings extra late summer visitors eager to take advantage of the low off season rates and airline specials. Jack arrived at the entrance to Orient Beach in his Suzuki jeep with the radio blaring rock and roll music and surveyed the parking situation. Taxi's, rental cars and restaurant workers from Le Village d'Orient filled the spaces along the road and under the trees near the Bikini Beach restaurant. Even the Village next to the beach was busy this beautiful morning. Constructed in classic French Creole Caribbean style in 2002 with multiple bright colors in the spirit of the 100+ year old homes still standing in the capital city of Marigot and Grand Case, the mixed atmosphere of restaurants, shops and housing to accommodate locals and tourists alike delighted the tourists who discovered it. Jack saw several couples of all ages and sizes as they walked past his car with beach towels under their arms focused on moving straight towards the water's edge. Eyeing what looked like a space large enough for his small vehicle, Jack spun the wheel and rolled slowly in the sand as Cheryl and Susan appeared from the shade of the beach bar. When he shut off the car, the Island 92 music was also silenced just as Bogart, the DJ, began his friendly chatter on the airwaves.

"Hi Jack!" yelled one of the women as he emerged from the vehicle and grabbed his towel and backpack from the passenger seat. "Turn that music back up! We love listening to Bogart's chatter. All we hear in the bar is the French techno stuff."

Turning toward the women, Jack yelled back "Do me a favor and do not yell Hi Jack in an airport or on a plane."

"Okay, we'll just say hi Mr. Jack. Now what about the music?"

"Besides, don't you know the music is played in the restaurants and bars for the waitresses and not for the customers!"

As he looked at the sea from the parking lot, Jack could see brightly colored catamaran sails, parachutes with happy tourists being pulled along the beach front by speed boats, and the rows of beach umbrellas covering comfortable cushioned lounge chairs. There was something about the fresh ocean scent that made his heart glad. *Not a bad lifestyle for a retired guy,* he thought.

"I thought you girls were headed to Club O again today for nude sunbathing."

"We did. And we do everyday. Thank goodness we extended our vacation! This island has proven to be more fun than we ever imagined. But girls don't live by sun and sex alone, big guy. We came to this end of the beach for some change of pace food. We hear the owner is from Baltimore and she flew in some Chesapeake Bay blue crabs." Susan explained with a smile. "Plus we were run off the beach by modesty when another load of tourists from the Cruise ship started walking the beach like deer in headlights amazed at naked sun bathers. It is so annoying that the cruise ship women walk the entire nude section wearing a one piece bathing suit while their husbands drool at the women on the towels. You would think that they could figure it out and show some skin to the old man."

Jack was now close enough to look deeply into the women's eyes. "Since when were you overcome with modesty?"

Cheryl interrupted, "Do you think I should get my clit pierced while I am here, Jack?"

Once again caught off guard by the women's playful approach to him, Jack considered the challenge of Susan's statement about married couples and ignored Cheryl piercing question. "You wouldn't believe what happens on the 4th of July. Parades of naked Americans from Club O walk the French beach singing patriotic songs and waving flags while celebrating a freedom that is against the law on almost all American beaches. There must be an irony there somewhere, but it escapes me at the moment. Now my mind is reeling. I think I must need a Cruzan rum and coke. By the way, you ladies look as good in bikinis as you do without them. Will you be my lunch dates today? We'll have a feast, drink too much and get crazy."

"Jack, we all need to loose 10 pounds or more. But what the hell? Lunch, then fun. We'll consider it an exercise program. What do you think, Cheryl?"

"Sweet. What a wonderful gentleman you are Jack." purred Cheryl. "Hopefully we will all stay awake long enough this afternoon for you take advantage of us after the food, the drinks and the beach."

"Yes, the thought crossed my mind. I stopped by to see my Auntie Em today so let's party all day." Jack announced playfully.

Cheryl looked at Susan with uncertainty. Susan spoke first, "He went to the ATM machine, get it? Don't be such a blonde, girlfriend." Both laughed again. "Tell us, Jack. Do you ever get Rock fever? We hear the local guys talk about it."

Jack quickly found his favorite table empty and pulled out the chairs for his dates. Resting comfortably across from them and glancing at the surf hitting the beach, he waved at his favorite waitress, Olivia, and ordered a rum and coke for himself and two BBC's for the girls. Waiting for the drinks to arrive, Jack moved the condiments around in the center of the table. "How big is your island? When I lived in New York, I rarely traveled outside of a 10 mile radius. My apartment was here, the office was here, my favorite bar was here, and most of my friends lived in this circle. Even the hospital where my wife died was less than 3 miles away from our home. My island was smaller than St. Maarten. For the most part, we all live on a self imposed island. We don't venture far. Our friends, our entertainment, our work are all close to the path we follow day by day. Anyone who thinks that a real island in the ocean is limiting, is wrong. People are tribal by nature and despite the opportunities presented by interstate highways, airplanes and boats most of us stay close to familiar people and places. Where you get your hair cut, where you visit the dentist, and where you leave your dry cleaning is always around the corner. That's why vacations are so important to us. If we can afford it, we break out. We change scenery. We try experiences and adventures beyond the routine of everyday."

Susan chimed in, "You can say that again!" Then a mischievous grin passed between the two women.

Cheryl looked directly at Susan then back at Jack, "Hey girlfriend! We seduced a philosopher! He's right. At home, you and I would be fighting over this wonderful man. Here we share. Sometimes you just have to escape. Perhaps we should go around the world later this afternoon!"

Jack was having a hard time remembering any moment when he was happier or more confused with feelings during the past two years. "You both should consider a return trip for New Year's Eve. Most of the restaurants on the beach stay open all night long. There are fireworks and crowds of people. In the morning, you can find hung over party animals passed out on the beach. I never saw anything quite like it when they counted down the ball at Times Square to welcome the New Year. This is definitely a new experience."

Now a questioning look passed between the two women, but neither of them spoke as they considered Jack's invitation.

The drinks arrived just in time to accent the moment so everyone raised their glasses in a toast and said, "Cheers!"

"Jack, do you think you will ever get married again?" asked Susan turning serious again for the moment.

"I hope so. But I know I am not ready … too many dreams of my lost wife. It would not be fair. How about you? You said that you are both divorced. Any plans to remarry?"

Susan responded before Cheryl. "My twelve year marriage to an absolute asshole was enough to keep me single for a while. I watched my weight and went to the gym twice a week. I listened repeatedly to his stupid jokes. I sat at the country club bar reading books while he spent endless hours on the golf course. I agreed to everything sexually he wanted. I had two children. I grew my career and made our household income flourish. He never appreciated a damn thing. Divorce suits me well. I need a break from that boring shit."

"Yeh, yeh, yeh. There are three sides to every divorce, my dear girlfriend. His story, your story and the truth. Don't forget you screwed the ski instructor in the lift going up the mountain at Aspen while you were on vacation with your husband" added Cheryl.

"And you sucked off your daughter's private English tutor in the parking lot of the junior high school, so don't throw stones." countered Susan. "Besides, didn't you see the Titanic movie? No one blamed the girl for screwing the boy in the cheap seats."

"Okay, TMI, TMI. This is definitely too much information!" Jack said as he held up his hands in surrender. Jack's cell phone rang and the Take Me Out to the Ball Game melody once again echoed from his pocket. Excusing himself, he stood and stepped a few feet toward the beach to answer the call away from the laughter and music of the restaurant. "Good Afternoon, this is Jack." He turned to the women so that they could hear his side of the phone conversation.

"Good Afternoon, Jack. It's me, J.R. Did I interrupt something?"

"Just the beginning of a great hangover … I am down on Orient Beach with a sexy blonde and a gorgeous redhead. Both are wearing very small bikinis. Both claim to be divorced so I believe them. The sun is shinning and the water is crystal blue. One of them just decided to pierce her privates. I might get to buy the first gold ring for her to use down there. How are you, my friend?"

Cheryl and Susan hugged each other and glowed from Jack's compliments. "Jack is such a flirt. We are ordinary looking and soon to be middle aged women. But this vacation and meeting Jack feels good to this old broad" offered Cheryl.

Jack ignored Cheryl and listened carefully to his cell phone.

"You dog. I'm at work trying to solve a murder. We got the autopsy report by email on that businessman from Front Street. A single 22 caliber bullet to the head killed him, just like we thought. Not a scratch on the body indicating any struggle. We know what he had for dinner and how much alcohol and marijuana he consumed in the preceding 4 hours before his death. And now we're fairly sure that the murder was not robbery related despite that his jewelry, money, and personal papers were missing. This one has to be another domestic violence episode, love triangle or revenge hit. It appears to be a murder of passion for sure."

"Why"

"The autopsy found fresh semen in his butt."

CHAPTER 15

▼

GUANA BAY, WHILE ANDY
IS IN HIDING

When the rain comes at night, the swaying trees and sounds of water on the tile terrace add another dimension to Caribbean living. Dana's constant wish was that showers would come every night between 2 AM and morning to nourish the plants and provide relaxing sounds for sleep. As she recognized the slight drop in temperature signaling the approaching front and warm rain shower, Dana strolled into the bathroom and dropped her shorts and top into the laundry basket. The entire home was built by an Italian architect, and Dana's master bath was no exception to his flair for the dramatic. With twelve foot ceilings, tile floors and walls, an open tub with an entire corner of the room used as an open shower, for Dana it was love at first sight. The toilet area was inside an enclosed water closet with a door at the far end removed from the dressing table and hand made pottery double sinks. Floor to ceiling mirrors had been mounted on two of the walls and there was a brightly lighted vanity mirror that stretched over the sinks. Several white wicker shelves with drawers and cabinet doors stored the towels, supplies and small appliances so common in everyone's bath. For maximum effect, the designer had placed many windows overlooking both the sea and the gardens surrounding the house. The outside spotlights illuminated the bath so well at night that Dana often used the room in the dark to enjoy the feeling of being in the garden. To further meld the bathroom with the outside, double

French doors opened to an enclosed courtyard of tropical flowering plants accented with a second outdoor shower. Accessible only through these doors, the area provided maximum privacy for the extra bathing area. The gray water created by the shower and the surrounding gutters was filtered and stored in a cistern that Andy and Dana used for the outside tasks like watering plants or washing the automobile.

Tonight, the rain would be perfect for using the courtyard shower. St. Martin temperatures rarely swing in extremes. Most of the year, days in the high 80's result in nights close to 80 degrees. Andy and Dana considered the outside shower to be the ultimate in tropical decadence. There was something special in standing under the lights of the sparkling stars. She gathered her favorite shampoo and a bottle of body wash then stepped naked through the French doors. A gecko scampered directly in front of her, and then moved up the wall to watch her as she turned on the hot and cold water facets. Without waiting for the hot water to reach the pipes, she stepped into the stream and shivered slightly. The refreshing cold shock of the initial flow of water was complimented by the beginning of more light rainfall. She turned around twice to enjoy the feeling of the bath water as it warmed before reaching for the shampoo. Then completely wet, she lathered her head and scrubbed her scalp as the soapy water twirled at her feet. Andy had installed two other shower heads at different angles and heights, so she switched on the valve that enabled them to rinse her head clean of the suds. Then she repeated the process for her entire body with the other soap. Two geckos now moved across the wall to take advantage of the water splashes. Friendly insects chirped in the bushes and the rain slowed to a fine mist.

There was a large brass rack filled with fluffy white towels just inside the doorway, and Dana grabbed one as she stepped inside. Leaving the door open, she quickly dried where she stood and wrapped the towel around her head. Andy had also built a small refrigerator into the bottom cabinets of one of the wicker stands to hold cold bottles of water for her night time cravings. She opened the door and grabbed a small plastic bottle. *So much for an exercise program. Andy doesn't even make me walk across the house for late night refreshment.*

Andy had been gone for three days. Despite Jack's assurances of his safety, waiting for this horror to end was maddening. Dana's only hope was to keep her life as normal as possible. Oddly, the policeman left behind in the driveway the day of the surprise visit disappeared in just a few hours, and the Inspector had only called again once to ask for Andy. The lack of pressure for Andy to appear for questioning was confusing, but welcome. She was having a hard enough time rationalizing her husband as a fugitive from the police. As long as she was left alone, she hoped that she could cope if events in the murder investigation moved to other clues.

Coby rested just outside the bathroom door, lying upside down which Dana found to be both odd and comical for a large dog. He balanced perfectly and watched the room while rubbing his back with slight motions and wiggles. She stepped over him still naked and crossed the room to her closet to find a robe. The loyal dog rolled over and followed.

"Come, come. Let's get a cookie."

Joyfully the dog stayed at her heals in anticipation of a dog treat from the kitchen. Dana crossed the large open living room to the kitchen bar and retrieved her wine glass from earlier that evening. Pausing at the pantry, she picked up the bag of dried chicken strips and Coby leaped playfully.

"You men are so easy."

Coby grabbed his treat from her hand and went to the corner. Dana heard the wind in the coconut palm trees as another cloud passed overhead and more rain fell. She moved closer to the open window to enjoy the sounds from the water hitting the pool and the edge of her covered terrace. Coby joined her once again. She patted his head and then moved outside to savor more of the water symphony as the drops danced on the foliage of the plants around the terrace and pool. She pulled one of her favorite chairs back so that the water could not reach her, and relaxed. The sea that dominated her view glistened in the moon light and more details became clear as her eyes adjusted to the darkness. She sat watching the ocean and heard the dog's nails click behind her. His less than dainty plop to the tiles to lie down near her produced a loud grunt.

"Yep, just like I thought earlier. You men are alike."

Coby only looked at her and yawned then he curled into a ball.

Dana watched as the cat scurried through the door to join them. *This is Paradise. I hope Andy comes home before I fall asleep.* The cat also plopped down next to Coby's head and immediately fell asleep.

Dana returned her attention to the ocean and saw another wave of rain pass the house. The water remained dark. Coby stretched at her feet, curled again and started to lick his penis.

"Okay, big boy … I stand corrected. Men and dogs are not exactly alike." Dana laughed. *I might not have a husband if men could do that. Yuck.* Her mind wondered and she thought of the joke her friend Betty used to tell the girls.

Two men were walking home from the car pool drop off in their suburban neighborhood one afternoon. As they passed a large yard, they heard growling and grunting. Looking towards the house they saw two dogs consumed in the sex act. As the dogs rolled, snorted and obviously enjoyed the coupling, one man spoke. " Damn, I miss that kind of spontaneous sex. My wife has become so boring in bed during our past few years. When we were younger it was like fireworks."

The other man replied, "You have to accept responsibility. It takes two in a relationship to make things work, you know. Have you brought home flowers lately? Do you greet her after a hard day of work with a Cosmopolitan martini instead of complaints and problems from your work?"

"You are right I haven't made the effort. What should I do?"

"Tonight mix a pitcher of martinis and watch the magic work. Nuzzle her neck. Nuzzle her breasts. Just watch those dogs. You'll see what I mean."

Several days passed and the episode was forgotten. Then another evening as they walked home, the two men saw the same dogs going at it with the same enthusiasm. The suspense started to drive the friend crazy so he stopped and asked his friend the result "Well, did you try my advice?"

"I did. Thank you. But it took 6 martinis for me to get her out into the front yard."

Dana smiled again at the old joke. Men and dogs. Dana loved them. She reached down and petted both of the animals.

It was time for a chilled glass of wine and a bite to eat, so Dana returned to the kitchen. This kitchen was her favorite place to putter in the house. With double gas ovens, a wrap around tiled counter top with space for every gadget, glass front upper cabinets and two huge sinks with a sexy faucet, she believed it was as pretty as the blue sea that surrounded the island. Even the pantry was so well organized and clean that she showed it off to friends who came for dinner. Opening the refrigerator, she picked a pear and an apple plus a block of cheddar cheese and placed them on a plate. After grabbing the open wine bottle and a sharp knife, she returned to the terrace. As her eyes adjusted to the night, she saw what must have been a small boat moving quickly across the water just off shore. Oddly, it did not have any running lights that she could see. From this distance, the noise of the engine or engines made a puttering sound but for the most part it was invisible to the homes on shore with all the people busy with dinner, favorite television shows, hot new books or the details of everyday life. Dana's imagination was sparked. *What are they doing on that boat in the dark of night? A drug run? Illegal fishing? Human smuggling? Disposing of a body?*

"Naw … they are probably like the people who drive without auto lights in the rain or after dark. Just plain stupid" she announced to no one.

Oh my god ... the only thing worse than drinking alone is starting to talk out loud to your self. I better finish eating and go to bed before Andy returns and finds me slobbering in a corner and claiming that Aliens abducted me for experiments.

With the cat and the dog following every move, Dana closed the house, secured all doors and went to bed. She left the outside lights and one light in the foyer on for Andy. After a quick stop in the bathroom, she dropped her robe next to the bed and slid under the covers. With the windows open on both sides of the master bedroom, the breeze from the comfortable night of light rain was all that she needed to slip off to sleep in minutes.

Half asleep, Dana rubbed the fresh sheets and pillow cases against her skin. Snuggling in this bed was one of her most luxurious past times. Since she and Andy always slept in the nude, her freedom of movement under the bedding was easy. She turned over and hugged her pillow as she drifted off again. The pressure of another body woke her when she tried to adjust the sheets to cover her bare shoulder. Andy was hogging the covers again, damn it. She tugged on the sheet just as a hand slipped between her legs. The fingers probed her pubic area awkwardly. Thinking that she must be in a strange position for Andy, Dana spread her legs to accommodate. Still the hand was groping and unfamiliar. Confused, Dana moved her hips to provide a more comfortable angle. But the hand was foreign. It was rough. And it pushed too hard against her vagina. She tried to sit up, but was pushed back down to the mattress with one forceful shove. Immediately, she smelled the sweat of a stranger. A stranger was in her bed and she was naked. *Where in the hell is Andy? Where in the hell is my dog?* She tried to roll over but she could not. The sheets were holding her down like a straight jacket. The panic of being trapped exploded in her brain and she forced out a scream, "Stop, stop!" But it was no use. Her heart was pounding. A second man was standing by the bed with his penis in his hand. He stroked it and put it inches from her mouth. She cried out again but neither man retreated. Pulling her legs into a bent position and bracing her arms, she mustered all the strength she could find and pushed her body upright. Her blood curling scream even terrified her.

Free to move, she snapped on the light next to the bed and suddenly felt foolish. The room was empty except for a startled and anxious dog staring at her.

CHAPTER 16

▼

JAMAICA, EARLY
SEPTEMBER

A few days after Cheryl and Susan gave Jack a tearful goodbye at the airport and returned home, Jack Donnelly traveled to Jamaica to attend a conference sponsored by the Retired Detectives Association. Not just a time to visit with old friends, this yearly event gave a feeling of unity and continuation to many retired men and women who had struggled with the day to day mysteries of murder crimes often without resolution, arrests or convictions by courts even when evidence was overwhelming. A recent change in bylaws had allowed practicing investigators to join the Association which was giving the break out sessions during conferences new focus on discussing, hypothetically of course, unsolved cases that needed a fresh approach or other objective thinking. Often, without interoffice egos or politics to consider, the facts of cases could be pondered in a more academic fashion and new ideas emerged.

After a full day of smiles, reunions, and the never ending sea of name badges that passed before his eyes, Jack slipped away from the first of many group banquet dinners to enjoy a fresh Dominican cigar and a tall dark rum and coke. Lighting his cigar, he strolled toward the garden and ocean access while he enjoyed the sudden quietness away from the dinner crowd. A soft breeze stirred the lush foliage of the garden as the usual chirping sounds of Caribbean insect life played the sweet melody of the dark night. Looking for place to sit and smoke,

Jack saw a white wall before him which led to a ramp with the greenish glow of a lighted pool behind it. Sensing a perfect opportunity to relax and watch the water away from interruption, Jack approached the top level of the ramp. As his vision adjusted to the brighter lights of the pool, Jack was greeted by three twenty something women and one man soaking in the pool. Completely naked, but huddled together in conversation as if in a business meeting in any boardroom, the four appeared to be slightly drunk and very happy. One girl appeared to be Asian, another Black, one White and he was not sure of the man's features. But then Jack didn't care about the other man anyway.

"Hey you!" cried out one of the three women. "Can you stop at the open bar on your left and bring me another Red Stripe?"

"Me too!" another woman called as she dove under the water and glided across the shimmering surface.

Jack watched her back and butt protrude seductively as she swam and crossed in front of him.

"Sure, ladies and gentleman. I live to serve." Jack replied clearing his voice with a slight cough, then reaching into a tub of ice cold beers he thought to himself, *I don't think the sedate dinner crowd in the banquet room has a clue about the pool party outside. Thank goodness.*

Turning from the bar to face the pool as one naked girl pulled her self out of the water Jack asked timidly, "Anyone else?"

Only friendly laughter came from the pool as Jack approached the stunning young woman carrying his rum and two beers in the traditional triangle with both hands and a cigar hanging from his mouth. This group was obviously enjoying catching the older Jack by surprise. Handing over the cold beers, Jack squatted to move closer to the three left in the pool and found himself at eye level with the naked girl's lower torso. A small red rose tattooed just to the left of her pubic area was less than three feet from his face. Turning and looking up, Jack stared in awe. "Nice Tattoo."

Without a missing beat or the slightest hesitation, the young black woman softly rubbed it and replied, "Body Art. My last employer did not allow any markings or tattoos to show when wearing business clothes so I picked this spot. What do you think?"

"I think that it probably makes you and your boyfriend very happy."

Immediately the girl reached out with her right arm and offered a traditional business handshake. "I am Rachel. What is your name? That cigar of yours smells great."

Oh great. A beautiful young naked woman wants to shake my hand and act like this is a fucking job interview or a cocktail party at the country club.

"Jack" was the only thing he could say.

"Well Jack, these are my friends. We're here celebrating a big marketing contract that we just signed and our boss sent us here to have some fun and escape the Northeast's cold weather this week. And it is okay if you look at my tits and my tattoo. After all, I did choose to be naked. And I work hard to keep my physique looking good Stop trying to be socially and politically correct. I am proud of my body. Two years ago I was overweight, sloppy and unhappy. Today I am very proud of my tits. You can check me out on my website or on YouTube." if you want.

Jack raised his rum glass in tribute, and gazed again at the others remaining in the pool all the time feeling just a bit out of place in full dress while this wild group remained without clothes or shame. Also he was confused by the tube she mentioned. What damn tube? His friends in high school used to call the television the tube. A few days ago in bed with Susan and Cheryl, he had felt 30 years old. Tonight, he felt 80.

"In fact, the guy in the pool is my boss. Say hello, Wendell" "Also the Asian looking girl on his right is Allison, his wife and the dumb blond with the sexy disgusting long hair and perfect figure is Michelle, my best friend. We all work together in Philly. The weather sucks back home, but this place is paradise! Now, why don't you join us? The warm evening is perfect for a skinny dip and the open bar is just steps away. What could be better to break the ice of meeting new people?"

"Who is the dumb blond now, Rachel? I don't look Asian. I am Asian. My mother and father were Asian. But then, what am I saying? You look black, but talk like a dumb blond" laughed Allison. Everyone applauded included Rachel.

"Well, I don't blame you. I blame your momma!" was Rachel's quick response.

Ignoring the women's banter and focusing on joining everyone in the pool Jack began looking around for a dry place to leave his clothes. "Well, I would usually say that I did not bring a swimming suit with me, but that answer would be a bit lame at this moment." He stood, kicked off his shoes then removed his shirt, pants and underwear and entered the pool behind Rachel. Taking his rum with him but leaving the cigar on the edge, Jack was amazingly comfortable with the casual nature of his new friends' abandonment of any social conventions.

This may be one of the stupidest things I have done in my life. Thought Jack. *The next thing you know I will probably be hanging on a fence at the airport back home being blasted by the jet thrust.*

Watching him disrobe, Michelle commented "Hey Jack, you take good care of yourself. How old are you?"

Best to answer a question with a question … Jack turned toward her and asked, "How old do I look?"

"Jack, we don't mean to be rude. Do you want to invite your wife to join us? I see you wear a wedding ring." announced the married girl, Allison.

Jack turned to face her. *In a good movie the hero always says a most perfectly timed response to defuse personal questions that he wants to avoid.* A long uncomfortable silence settled over the group. Jack looked at his left hand then took another sip of the rum and coke.

"I wish I could." Jack replied quietly. "My wife died a few years ago. Breast cancer. Too young. Too soon. There were so many things we plan to do … some day. I miss her. And I usually prefer to say nothing. But it seems unnatural and completely out of place not to tell you given the rather unusual circumstances of this evening. Secrets are hard to keep with four new naked friends!" After a long pause he added, "I hope that I did not bring sadness to you this evening by telling you."

Wendell replied immediately before the others could speak. "Jack, life is fragile. We may be young, dumb, and without the experiences you're had but we do know that there are times to have fun and times to be serious. Some of our friends even consider us over the top at times but your use of the term someday reminds me. My calendar has Monday, Tuesday, Wednesday on it but not a Someday. Thank you for your honesty. We know others who have died too young from breast cancer. Little by little, progress is made. More people are aware. More research succeeds in finding prevention and cures. Less people hide or deny symptoms, and knowledge gives more women a chance."

Suddenly everyone was silent as they remembered someone they loved and lost. Then Michelle interrupted their thoughts with "Enough of this sad shit, you two. We are here to have some fun! Here's to breasts! Here's to new friends! Here's to the happiness of today."

Everyone looked at each other, wiggled in the water and raised their drinks as Jack called out, "Here is to Birthday suits!" Everyone laughed and continued to splash about in the water as two heads appeared at the edge of the wall. Cautiously, another young man and woman entered the pool area and surveyed the inhabitants of the pool. You could almost see them counting: They looked carefully at the 2 men plus 3 women. Seeing that not one of the parties in the pool was wearing a swim suit both smiled approval at the group and waved hello. Instantaneously, both new comers stripped off their resort dinner clothing and pranced over to the bar area. After fixing what looked like rum punch, they slid into the water and moved quickly toward Jack. They beamed as they approached him and kissed and touched each other like new lovers on the morning after.

"Where are you folks from?" The new woman, a chubby brunette, asked as she threw her arms around her mate and bounced playfully in the 4 foot water.

Jack politely answered, "These folks are from Philly and I am from New York but now St. Martin. Where are you from?"

"Minneapolis, we arrived this morning. We just got married!"

Pausing with some surprise, Jack asked "When, exactly, did you get married?"

As the young man took another sip of his rum punch, he hugged his new bride with his free arm and stood triumphantly behind her. A vision of the American classic rural couple flashed in front of Jack's mind and he expected to see the guy hold a pitch fork. This couple was very ordinary looking and their features screamed normal. Except, of course, that they were naked. Both man and woman gazed at each other and replied in unison, "10 o'clock this morning" as they proudly held up their left hands and displayed the new shinny gold bands.

Rachel screamed, "How cool you guys! Married at 10 AM and naked with complete strangers only 12 hours later." Everyone applauded again.

The new bride explained, "You know. I probably will never see you again. But someday when I sit on my porch in a rocking chair with my grandchildren I know that I will have a memory that puts a smile on my face. Life does not have to be boring or without fun. Today, I have Jamaica. Tomorrow, we never know. I plan to have wonderful memories of this wedding. Now tell me more about St Martin and about Philadelphia and about the many wonderful things that wait for us. I want to do as much as possible all in my married life! This is not the beginning of settling down; this is the beginning of many new adventures." Then she hugged her new husband.

As the now more intoxicated group refreshed their drinks and jumped in and out of the pool, a slightly older couple came up the ramp and like the newly weds, carefully counted the boy-girl ratio once they determined that everyone was without any proper bathing attire. After talking privately to each other at the bar as they selected some drinks, they too shed all clothes and quickly joined everyone in the pool. The woman was blonde and lean. The man had dark short hair and looked like tennis pro. Jack now was relieved that finally someone over 40 was joining the party. *Thank goodness. I was feeling like a lecherus old man sur-*

rounded by nubile twenty year olds. At least this couple is older. But then, one guy brought 3 women, one guy has a new bride, and one guy has his 40 something stunning girlfriend or wife. I am alone. This sucks. Whatever became of spin the bottle? At least everyone had a chance.

The blonde broke the silence. "Hello Everyone! You look marvelous."

Cheers of welcome sounded in unison and smiles were exchanged.

Drinks flowed and conversation continued as everyone drifted from person to person in the pool meeting and greeting. Jack wondered if he had somehow stumbled into a naked United Nations meeting. For Jack, whatever this strange encounter turned out to be, it was better than being shot at in a big city by vicious criminals, better than being threatened by politicians when his investigations hit a nerve or sensitive subject, and definitely a step above sitting lonely back in his apartment with Stray Cat. Jack left the pool and poured another Cruzan rum and coke. Oddly, he found the ice well full and the entire pool bar completely stocked for the night. Without a bartender, it would seem that the pool bar would be ignored by the hotel staff. Apparently it was not. He suspected that there had been a history of naked parties most nights. As he returned to the pool, Jack was greeted by the exit of his four original pool friends. They started gathering clothes indicating that they would not return. Only the two couples remained in the water. Suddenly Jack was the odd man out and was very reluctant to reenter the water.

Rachel turned to get the group's attention, "Jack and the rest of you naked shameless people! Thank you so much. But I have to take my drunken friends back to their rooms because tomorrow we change hotels and move to Hedonism. It was so nice to meet you!" The three women and man collected all clothing, dressed, and walked away just as the 40 something guy pulled himself out of the pool and announced that he was in search of a bathroom. This left the newly wed couple, Jack and the lone 40 something woman with an opportunity to quietly wish each other a good night. The bride was first to exit and pull her new husband behind her. They gathered their belongings and hugged again. Then the naked newly weds stumbled away, laughing and groping each other with their clothes in hand, Jack turned to the lone blonde woman who now moved through the water to the edge of the pool.

"Looks like we are finally alone … my name is Theresa. No need for you to get dressed yet. The night is still young. You aren't drunk are you?"

Jack stared for a moment looking around expecting the man she arrived with earlier to reappear. Then, he spoke. "Where is your husband or boyfriend? I thought he told us he was going to find a bathroom."

"We will get to that later, Jack Donnelly. For now, I just want to get to know you better." She pulled herself out of the pool and stood directly in front of him. Next, she softly ran her hands from his neck down his chest circling his abdomen as she moved closer to his body with hers. Suddenly they were almost touching and he could smell her hair fresh with chlorine from the pool. "Chris is not coming back to the pool. He called it a night. Now it is just you and me, Jack. Please don't run away afraid. I do not bite. I promise. Chris and I are attending the conference. Well, actually I am an investigator with the force in Dallas and he came to play some golf and enjoy the sun. Chris works in IT for a large insurance company. We have a great and ordinary life in the burbs. Two children doing well in high school, a comfortable home, and more charge cards than we should … typical Americans I guess, except we have never been divorced. This conference gives me a chance to listen to some of the retired pros in our business. You are well known, Jack. I saw you earlier and asked a bit about you. Then Chris and I talked about it during dinner and we decided that we want you to come up to our room for some fun. My fantasy has always been to make love with two men at once. After all, we are on vacation!"

Jack blushed. *There you have it. Hollywood movies and fiction novels often understate the real danger. Women prey on men. Jack, my boy, go back to your hotel room and save yourself. Now Jack. You can do it.*

"Theresa, I think you may be taking this concept of an all inclusive vacation to a new level."

She posed briefly like a model and faked a pout that quickly turned to a smile. "Please don't say no."

Touching her shoulders, Jack took a moment to slowly look at the naked woman before him in the glow of the pool lights. The classic girl next door, shapely and a well proportioned size 6, Theresa had the figure of the younger girls who had just left the pool. Fresh out of the water, she was not wearing makeup or sexy clothing. But she was as sensual and desirable as a movie star. For the next few moments they simply looked into each other's eyes. Then as she scooped up their clothes with the other hand and pulled on his arm to lead him through the garden. She whispered, "Come on Jack." Ahead he could see the flicker of a soft candle light burning on the nearest terrace. With some hesitation, he followed her. Turning at the open door, she kissed him as he stepped into the darkened hotel room.

Didn't I see a male prostitute do this in some movie about a gigolo when he went to the home of a rich couple … then he was set up for the wife's murder later?

CHAPTER 17

▼

JAMAICA, THE NEXT MORNING

Jack rolled over in the hotel room bed and quickly oriented himself to the surroundings. Even though the curtains were closed in this ground floor room, he could tell that the sun was up and that there was a woman lying next to him curled in a spoon fashion with her back to his chest. The air conditioning hummed in the background. Looking around without moving his head, it appeared to Jack that they were alone in the room. An involuntary yawn slipped out of his mouth and the woman stirred.

"Are you awake, Jack?"

"Yes, Theresa. What time did we fall asleep?"

"It was after 4 AM, I think." She shifted and pushed her body closer to his. "Chris had an early Tee time, so he left us just after 6 AM. I would have ordered us coffee and fresh fruit juice but I was not sure how long you would sleep. Are you hungry? Do you need some coffee?"

"No, my role in your night of fantasy will probably keep me going for a several hours. I think my adrenaline may be off the Richter scale right now."

"Oh Jack, don't be dramatic. You men can be so serious at times. It was only sex. Great sex. But only sex."

"Well, I can't say that being over 50 is boring. That's for sure."

Theresa stood and grabbed her pillow. "I am ordering coffee and a plate of fruits from room service. You are invited to stay for breakfast." Then she threw the pillow at his head and lifted the phone receiver.

As he left the bed, Jack found his clothing from last night's pool party on a nearby chair and took them into the bathroom. He relieved himself, stepped into the shower for quick refreshment, and then slipped on his pants and shirt. Walking barefoot from the bathroom, Jack found the terrace curtains and door open. Theresa sat around a small table wearing a bathing suit and brushing her hair. He took the chair opposite her and was at a loss for words. This was an unusual morning.

"Jack, I heard that you gave up the excitement of New York for an island in the Caribbean. Is that true?"

"Yes, after my wife's death I needed to get away. Some people throw themselves into work when they loose a loved one. Some fall into depression. With no children or immediate family to consider, I decided to move to warmer weather. When we were married we visited St Martin once on a cruise ship so I went there. I wanted to experience those wonderful memories again. It was a good choice. I haven't found a reason to leave."

Theresa waved to the young man approaching the terrace with a room service tray. She looked back at Jack. "Do you work?" Then she smiled at the waiter, said "Good Morning" and accepted the tray by placing it on the table between them. The waiter returned the greeting and quickly slipped away to respect their privacy.

"Interesting that you ask about my ability to work, Theresa. I live in a Foreign Country. Most Americans never consider my legal status when they talk to me and discover that I live on an island. They simply assume that I can move, work, start businesses, or do what ever the heck I want just like in the United States. They have heard about Green Cards and illegal aliens at home, but they somehow fail to make the rules apply to me or to themselves. I know it sounds naive, but most of them look at me like I am crazy when I tell them that I am as illegal as any Mexican or Cuban crossing into Texas without permission. They just don't get it. Bar conversations with tourists always turn into questions of how to get a job that pays well or the cost of housing. No one asks how long they would be allowed to remain in a foreign country without a permit or a visa. It is just not a part of the American reality. Somehow we seem to believe that the world is our oyster."

Theresa poured them both coffee and added cream to her cup. "But isn't it different for the rich and famous?"

Jack laughed and drank his coffee black. "Yes, it is always different for the rich, famous or talented. Think about the Cuban baseball stars who defect to the USA. They have visa for their families in hand at lightning speed. I doubt that any Caribbean islands turn away many millionaires. Remember the Playboy Playmate who made the Bahamas her home before she died? The press had photos of the Minister of Immigration kissing her at a bedside."

"Yes, I remember. Do you think that my tits would qualify me for a residency permit?"

"No comment, Officer" replied Jack as he poured more coffee into their cups.

Theresa leaned forward and touched Jack's leg. "So Jack Donnelly, how do you keep busy? Hiding from Immigration raids?"

"No. I made friends with the police on both sides of the island by offering free counsel from time to time. The science of forensics is non existent because of budgetary concerns and most investigations involve asking lots of questions and following up rumors rather than hard physical evidence. The islands don't even have credit reports never mind data bases of finger prints and DNA. Life is simpler. It has it's good points and then it has frustrations. Maybe it is like the Wild West. I am not sure. But for me it is a unique opportunity to stay under the immigration radar. As a matter of fact, I was called to an investigation of a murder victim recently."

"No kidding." Theresa asked with sudden interest. "What happened?"

"Investigator, you can not help yourself. Can you? Suddenly I see your pulse quicken" replied Jack as he shifted in the chair and looked over the garden before them.

"Jack, last night my pulse quickened. Now I am a willing student. Tell me about the damn murder."

"Okay, okay ... you are at least 10 years younger than me and probably could take me in a fair fight, so I better cooperate. Here is what I know. An American living on the island was found in the back seat of his car with a single 22 bullet in his head. No sign of struggle but also the body and glove compartment had been picked clean. No ID, no car papers, no Residency Permit, no cash, and no personal jewelry left on the victim. An officer on the scene remembered a conversation in a brothel between two men that seemed to threaten the life of a local merchant. It involved money owed for an attack."

"What? You have whorehouses on the island?" asked Theresa in shock.

"Do you think that islands have the only people who have sex for money businesses? Are you kidding? I will give you the tourist guide talk later, for now, let's stick with the investigation as I remember the details."

"Sorry."

"Now, this guy had plenty of rumors circulating around town because of his behavior. First the bad guys in the brothel were pissed at him. Then he had a law suit against a former business partner, also an American. Supposedly he sent a team of men to threaten the couple in the law suit and drive them off the island. Home invasion attacks have run off other families. But this time the couple fought back. The police are fairly certain that the couple had the motivation to kill him. Or at least the husband did. The wife was home alone and rumor has it that the guys sent to do the job stripped her naked then enjoyed some unscheduled fun. Who knows? I know them and talked to them after the incident, but there was probably information they withheld from me. They were traumatized and dealing with many emotional mood swings. There was never a police report filed by the couple."

"Well, it does sound like the male egos of either of the suspects could have motivated a murder. Want more coffee? I am going to order a pitcher of Mimosas. This sounds more interesting than your immigration stories."

"Male egos? Remember, I resemble that remark." interjected Jack. "Okay, enough immigrant stories for now. We will concentrate on this murder investigation. Order me a bucket of Carib beers. If they don't have them get me Corona, and please ask for extra limes!"

Theresa walked back to the phone to place the order with room service.

While Jack waited on the terrace, some clouds moved over the palm trees and a light sun shower sprinkled the tropical plants in front of him. He heard some laughter from female voices just over the next group of rooms and smelled the distinctive fragrance of marijuana float by with the breeze. He let a soft sigh escape his lips. Considering that he had been in bed with this woman and her husband just hours before, Jack felt strange, but somehow considered her a long time friend.

"I'm back. Did you miss me?"

Jack looked up as Theresa returned to her chair. "You and Chris are certainly a new experience for me. Hell, I have never made love to a woman with another man in the room. Never mind the fact that it was her husband."

"I hope that you enjoyed yourself. I certainly did."

"You made both men feel special and wanted from my point of view. Was this the first time you ever did this?"

"Yes, Jack. It was. Believe it or not, we are not swingers. When Chris asked me what I wanted for my birthday this year, I told him my fantasy. This is not something that I could ever do at home given my employment status and role in the community. So when we saw you at the opening cocktail party, he actually suggested that I talk to you. We knew from others that you were here alone."

Jack shifted in his chair, feeling somewhat stalked.

Theresa continued, "Chris is an exceptional man, sex partner, and husband. We married young and grew up together. We share everything. I have no secrets from him. But don't try to get off the subject, Jack. Let's hear what you know about this murder."

"Someday are you going to let him bring home another woman?"

Theresa shook her head and waved her finger. "Back to the murder subject, my detective friend. We can discuss more sex later."

The second room service order arrived and once again Theresa served the drinks and expected Jack to continue with the details of his investigation.

"You should know that I have a friendship with the couple who were attacked. I went to the house the morning after the incident. While they did not tell me all the details of the evening as I said earlier, I know that there were some sexual threats made by the men who came to scare them. The husband arrived after the men were in the house and was able to surprise them. I know that the wife was able to grab the gun during the scuffle. I know that shots were fired. I also know that the husband, Andy is his name, was mad as hell. The police know about my friendship with them but they still suspect him as a primary suspect."

"Let's think about this ..." Theresa analyzed with an official tone. "Forget about a lawsuit or business problems. Someone sends goons into your home. They probably strip and fondle your wife. You are going to find the bastard who planned it. At first he may have wanted to get even with a threat but emotions got out of hand and bam, the guy is dead."

"I know. And Andy had the weapon to do it. Dana, his wife, kept the gun from the attack." shrugged Jack as he removed his shirt and picked up a beer from the iced bucket. "Wow, they had some Coronas. Usually they only want to serve Red Stripe beer in Jamaica since it is made here. I must be lucky this trip."

Theresa thought for a moment about the couple's situation and probable guilt. "It looks like a slam dunk from my perspective, except for my experience" said Theresa as she looked at her mimosa and rubbed the condensation on the side of the glass.

"What?" asked Jack. "What did you run across with a strong motive like this one?"

"Well, we had a murder of a pretty young socialite wife outside of Dallas. Trust fund on her side of the family, husband in the wealth management business but struggling financially, no children, rumors of wild swimming pool parties with swinging couples, and the wife's insulting remarks to the husband in front of guests. Rumors that he had fallen in love with another woman. Sounded like the typical husband kills wife episode ... Scott what's his name replayed. He even left the country for a retreat one week after the funeral. My office was ready for his head. It seemed obvious. We just needed to find a murder weapon to tie him to the case. He did not have an alibi at the time of the murder. She was gunned down in a shopping mall parking lot and the damn security cameras were not working! No one saw anything until a passing security guard stopped to check the open door of the car. The husband stood to inherit the trust plus a large insurance policy. She had been a real bitch. No one in my office needed more evidence of motivation for him to have killed her. But it turned out that her best girl friend shot her. Yep. The woman evidently fell in love with her. Wanted her to leave her husband. Start a new life. When she was rejected, boom! The girlfriend killed the woman she loved and could not have. Who was to know? Even the husband was in the dark."

Theresa adjusted her chair and placed her foot in Jack's lap.

"Oh, oh. Now you are telling me that your jealous husband will appear and shoot me."

"No. I am telling you that you are very lucky you did not reject me last night." Jack looked at her foot in his lap.

"Just kidding, Jack!" Theresa wiggled her foot for attention. "Now back to the murder on St. Maarten. What happened after the couple was identified by the police as suspects?"

"There is more, naturally. The murdered guy had plenty of people he pissed off. There was a pretty blonde working for him that he flaunted around town from time to time. Grabbing her butt, getting too close in public, the usual stuff. Except this blonde had a well known live-in boyfriend. There were several incidences at bars or on the main street of town to make the local bartenders, waitresses and waiters wary of violence when the three showed up together. Mix in alcohol, male egos, and touching someone's girlfriend under the table in public and you often get trouble. But wait, there's more! When the police checked the murdered guy's voice mail, the only messages were from an anxious sounding French male. Just days before the murder, he called begging for a return call from this guy Nat over 12 times. And here is the real shocker ... the autopsy found semen in the dead man's butt. The report concluded that he had sex just an hour or so before his death. No sign of rape or violence on the body."

"Wow. That is surprising shit! Do you think the male sex partner killed him?"

"Not likely, because the body was fully dressed. Why have sex, then get dressed … then argue and pull out a gun?"

"I disagree. It sounds reasonable to me. More than one lover has killed the other." commented Theresa as she handed Jack a fresh cold beer and topped off her Mimosa. "What did the police learn when they questioned the French guy?"

"Nothing. They never found him. He left the island during the week after the murder before the police even heard the voice mail messages. No evidence to chase after him. Friends say that he left on a sailboat for Martinique but again no one knows for sure. Islands close together provide easy escape routes."

Theresa thought for a moment then replied, "Martinique sounds French so this guy would not need permission to be there … correct? We seem to be back to your immigration and legal status discussion."

"You got it. Colonialism lives as long as the original ruling nations provide funding and leave the local politicians alone. The USA has influence in some island territories in addition to the mother countries. Remember when the US invaded Grenada? Just recently the Associated Press reported that this country, Jamaica, is trying to improve its standing with the USA on the issue of trafficking and exploitation of people. Money and other benefits are at stake. The US State Department has a rating system. Tier 3 classifications subject the island nation to US sanctions including a loss of some forms of aid. Jamaica just moved to the Tier 2 level."

"I hate to sound like a movie trailer, but follow the money, Jack. You just might solve your murder."

"You are on target, Madame Detective. The police found over $600,000 in cash in the dead man's apartment. And a receipt for the purchase of a Go Fast boat typically used by human smugglers or drug runners. Other rumors around the island put this guy in the company of many late night folks with less than stellar reputations. I keep thinking how organized the crimes of human smuggling and drugs can be with the stakes involved. A connection to the murder is probable."

"Jack, you may need a gun if you get tagged by the wrong people."

"I won't discount your theory, but often guys like this murdered man are simply in the chain and most of the money is owed to others. He may have just been a collection point and was killed at the wrong time. The Public Prosecutor has the money now, not me. But I will keep your warning under advisement. I really don't need that kind of shit storm at this point in my life."

"You may not want to hear this but … also don't discount your friends' involvement in the murder. Anger is a great motivator. I know you like the couple, but either of them could have pulled the trigger." Theresa added.

"Yes, but there is a long list of possible murderers … now that homosexuality has entered the picture, the heat on the police from Government is cooling to solve the murder."

Theresa looked at Jack with a puzzled face. "What are you talking about?"

"Simple. Caribbean culture is strong on the man-woman sex thing. When the police are called to issues of family abuse they often take the man's side over the woman's. When homosexuals are involved it gets worse. Two gay men were beaten badly with a tire iron outside of a well known tourist attraction. Little was done by police. Until it surfaced that the men were well connected with a major USA Network news show, that is. Then some heads began to roll. The business of tourism was suddenly on the line. All the perpetrators were arrested and brought to trial. Funny how justice can work at times."

"Oh, God. Tell me that is not true."

"It is true. The reality is that this murder investigation may just quietly slip away. No tourist harmed. No BH degreed family talking to the press because a family member's murder is going unavenged. The US press is not even interested. There is just one dead gay guy who was an immigrant and he was a nasty bastard at that."

"Jack, again you confuse me. I understand the homosexual prejudice issue exists in some cultures. I understand the protection of tourism. There are few newspapers today that don't have at least one editorial or article about illegal immigrants. But what the hell is a BH degree?"

Jack picked up his beer and drank. "BH stands for born here. Voters. People with a political voice. Just like in the States, voters make a difference in democratic societies. Especially on small islands that control who can vote. My guess is that this murder investigation will slip away because no one really gives a shit about this guy."

"Oh." Teresa was appalled.

Jack reached for her hand. "Actually, I am not sure that is a bad thing in this case."

▼

CHAPTER 18

GUANA BAY, IMMEDIATELY AFTER THE POLICE VISIT

When Andy left his home in flight barely escaping the surprise visit from Inspector Holiday, he headed for the beach through the vacant lots of the neighborhood after stopping and calling Jack for advice. To his horror, he found out that he was susceptible to interrogation and possibly being held for weeks during the murder investigation without being charged. He thanked God that Dana had convinced him to keep that noisy dog. *"Coconut Retrievers are beautiful animals"* he thought with a new fondness for the animal. Jack had carefully explained that in a foreign country there is seldom a quick release of suspects held for questioning in serious crimes. Most frequently they are not initially charged, just held. Especially non-nationals. *Tourists who steal in the Caribbean when visiting on Cruise Ships must either be crazy or incredibly stupid.* A bougainvillea plant brushed his shoulder and cut his arm with its thorns. *Ouch. Running from police sucks! I'm too old for this shit. I've got to get across the boarder to the French side fast.*

Feeling an increased sense of paranoia, Andy remembered the story of the vacationing Wisconsin school teacher who swallowed a 3 carat diamond ring just as the sales lady turned her head in a well known Island jewelry store. When the alert salesperson noticed the ring missing it only took her anguished cry to summons security agents. They swooped down, the manger was called and the guy was pushed into an empty office. Held in the room despite his indignant protests, at first he sat coolly in front of a large flat screen monitor while the manager replayed the digital recording of the ring case surveillance camera so that she could find the activities surrounding the missing ring. After about ten minutes of replay that showed scenes of happy shoppers, she found it. There he was clear as a bell on the big screen in full HD color and with one quick and sneaky motion he moved the ring to his mouth. She could even see him swallow. Once the damning incident was identified, the man's cocky demeanor showed signs of strain. He stammered, he cried, he feigned outrage but the manager only asked that he open his mouth for her so that she could stick in her fingers and feel around. Hoping that it would let him off, he allowed her probing. Instead, satisfied that he had the ring in his stomach, the store manager called the police and requested immediate assistance. For the next hour the man was kept in the same room watching the recording being played over and over for visiting members of the press, police, tourist office officials and ship's officers from the visiting cruise line. A defense was pointless.

Arrested and taken to the police station, the now terrified middle class thief was hurried to a plain cell with no window, sink, toilet or bed. After he was order to undress and told to sit naked in the corner, a large silver bedpan was brought to the cell. Quickly the arrested man figured out that they intended to recover the stolen ring and have the evidence once nature took its course. A man in uniform placed a comfortable chair across from the cell bars with a full view of the small area and offered his prisoner any fast food, alcohol or water that he might want to hasten the process. After 9 miserable hours of refusing food and drink, he requested a cheese burger, fries and some cold beer. Unfortunately constipation set in and the thief had to sleep sitting up on the floor against a bare wall. A light remained on in his cell all night long and the guards changed every 7 hours so that someone could monitor his every move. Late the next morning after a large plate of greasy scrambled eggs and bacon plus several cups of luke warm coffee, relief was mixed with a severe case of humility. The now disgusting pan was pushed through the bars into a waiting container. The guard on duty sealed it in a plastic bag and handed it to a waiting representative summoned from the jewelry store.

"Can I have my clothes back now?" asked the prisoner.

"No, mon."

"Come on. You got what you wanted. Just let me have my clothes. I have rights. Someone is going to pay for this" yelled the red faced and angry thief.

"Yeh, mon. Someone's gonna pay for sure. Antillean lawyers on this island ain't cheap."

Still naked and feeling defeated he returned to his corner and shut up. After 3 additional days and two more repeated episodes of fecal removal from the bare cell to make sure the man had not managed to steal more than one ring, he was finally given his clothes then moved to a cell with a bed, a toilet, and three other rather mean looking and unbathed men. After a quick glance at the single bunk and the three men in the cell, the now infamous ring sw allower had had enough. He passed out and crumpled to the floor.

*   *   *   *

Andy continued down the beach toward the French border trying to put as much distance between himself and the police as he could without running. *Exercise is great. However, moving by foot when you have to travel fast is the pits.* He approached the open sand and removed his polo shirt so that he could blend in as another tourist taking a healthy walk. Luckily he had been wearing cargo shorts in the yard with boat shoes. The shorts had lots of pockets and they contained credit cards, a cell phone, and cash. He knew that a chase or any organized effort to find him was unlikely. Jack speculated that the police would simply station an officer at the driveway to the house and wait for his return to Dana later that day. Continuing his escape, he found that the sand became wider and he was further away from the protection of nearby foliage. Feeling more exposed, he turned back up the hill away from the sea slightly. Just ahead was a shuttered building that housed a beach bar opened a year ago by a Canadian Couple but now closed due to the off season. Rumor was that the couple had held successful high powered careers for many years then followed their dreams to the islands. Appropriately, they named the bar the "Former Life Bar and Grill". Using a kind of crazy theme approach, they had decorated the entrance lobby with mannequins dressed in easily recognizable outfits and uniforms of known careers. One shapely female form was dressed as a nurse, there was a business executive mannequin dressed in a dark blue suit with a white shirt and red tie complete with brief case, and even a topless woman figure in a thong with a gold chain that read: "Former Porn Star." Above the display was a banner with the words: "Dear Boss … I'm calling in well. Can't make work today. Sorry, I have gone Coconuts!"

Unfortunately, with no hotel or high density population in this residential beachfront neighborhood, the bar was not a money maker. With no reputation and no active advertising campaign, the area was overlooked and few tourists made their way to this destination. It was clear that the owners' former lives of career success did not include marketing skills or wise business decisions that studied demographics or island traffic patterns.

Feeling somewhat tired and disheveled, Andy paused for a moment under one of the bar's multi-level outdoor terraces and checked the parking lot for any police cars. Only three local cars and one rental jeep with day visitors to the nearly deserted beach could be found. Relieved, Andy looked around the old building remembering the last visits he and Dana spent during a few happy hours in the bar inside. With a sigh, he started to leave and almost bumped into a man who suddenly appeared near some of the propane tanks on the side of the building.

"Whoops! Sorry, I didn't see you. I was thinking about the last time my wife and I visited this bar ..."Andy mumbled slightly embarrassed. *The Fugitive needs to pay more attention.*

"Eh?" His Canadian accent was pronounced. "No problem, guy. I'm the owner and I was just taking pre-season look around the place" answered the man. "My wife is in Canada visiting family and we probably will return to open in late November. It is good to hear that you have been here. Do you vacation or live here? We really appreciate the business."

"Don't you have anyone looking after it for you?"

"Not really. The labor force is not exactly full of local workers for bars and our staff last year never did receive approval for work permits. At least my wife and I are directors in our company so we could work legally. Otherwise, some nights we would not have had anyone to keep the place open during the last high season!" sighed the man.

"Well, great to meet you. We live in the neighborhood" said Andy hoping to cheer the man's mood. "Our home is on the other end of the beach and you know how it goes ... we don't always get down to this end. Sounds kind of stupid, actually, as I say it. Sorry we have not met in the past. I am Andy Parkerson. My wife is Dana. We are from the USA and moved here to help a friend. Long story. But we love this island, we love the Caribbean people, and we love the challenges."

"I can't believe anyone would love the challenges, but nice to meet you too, Andy. My name is Tim. Come on in. I was just going to take a moment for a cold drink and check things out. Let's see how dusty the Former Life Bar has become in the past two months."

"You have the place full of booze?" asked a startled Andy.

"Goodness no. I trust the wooden shutters and hurricane covers to a point but not that much! When we closed for off season we removed all supplies. See my cooler by the door? I brought some ice cold beers with me."

Andy momentarily forgot about the police and his trip to the French side. "Sounds like a plan. Let's check it out." Both men started up the stairs to the empty wooden deck and front doors covered by closed storm shutters. Andy waited patiently as Tim unlocked the heavy metal mechanism, released the bolt and raised the iron bar that crossed the door. Then he released latches that secured the two sections of thick wooden shutters and pulled them apart. After fiddling with the keys, he found the door deadbolt key and opened the wooden framed glass French doors. The smell of musty air greeted the men as they entered.

"Hang on Andy whilst I find the electrical panel and give us some power. I wouldn't want you to end up on top of my pretty Porno Star in the dark!"

Andy was quick to call out as the other man walked into the dark, "I have seen her draw the whole bar crowd's attention as a drunken tourist momentarily mistook her for real. Hell, I thought about jumping her bones too after 4 of your famous rum and cokes."

"Nothing wrong with a fantasy, my friend." The room came into focus as several switches in the back sounded and Tim asked, "How is that? Enough for us to see without tripping over stuff?"

"Good to go."

"Alright let's get a few windows open and let the sun shine in. Plus we need the ventilation." Tim crossed the room and started releasing the security bars from the inside of each window facing the sea. "Did you notice the American Bill of Rights in the Porn Star's right hand? That was Mary's idea. She's my wife and partner in the venture. Actually most of the unusual decorations and humorous stuff for our bar were her ideas back when she was excited about this insanity."

Andy joined in opening windows and pushing the exterior shutters to each side smelling the fresh ocean air. *This sure beats sitting in the Philipsburg Police station! I wonder if that captured school teacher who stole the diamond had a new respect for teaching the Bill of Rights back home after his release?* Now that the dark corners of the room were lighted, Andy looked around and saw the familiar Nurse and Business Executive mannequins in place. Richly paneled, the room had the appearance of a fishing village pub complete with various used boat equipment items, ceramic fish, nets, and the obligatory T-shirts, bikini tops, and ladies underwear stapled to the walls behind the bar. Most were signed by the donators.

Tim interrupted Andy's thoughts. "Sadly, the dream of owning a bar in Paradise and the reality of working day to day with new challenges soured Mary a bit. She will be a tough sell to convince her that we should return this season. Get us a couple of beers, Eh?"

Andy reached for two cold Carib beers in the cooler and was surprised to see a zip lock bag full of cut lime wedges. "Tim, you are the man! I compliment your attention to detail. What happened?"

Both men grabbed a chair and turned towards the open windows propping their legs against the window sills. Just as they moved into a comfortable position, three attractive 50 something women walked by on the shoreline and waved to them.

"Good morning, Ladies!" Tim called out.

"Now, talk about a rainbow of beauty … one black, one white, and one with that beautiful mixed skin of multi-culture. Life is good" noticed Andy as he suddenly missed Dana.

"The creator certainly had a few surprises in store for men with the whole package!" said Tim as he sipped his beer. "Ironically Mary was the leader in our decision to give up the life at home for island time. Until the emotional events and constant illogical challenges pushed her beyond the point of recovery, that is. Our first challenge was with establishing a company called an N.V. to operate the business. After the 911 attacks and the drop in business in the Caribbean things appeared to move more efficiently here because of the pressure to restore the island's economy. We only waited about 9 months for our paperwork and approvals. We heard that it can take years."

"Yes, I have some experience with the horrendous red tape and demand for additional documentation at every turn. Once, it took me nine separate government office visits to give them $175 for a change of address certificate. Type A personalities can never live in the islands, that's for sure. We even waited for one year when applying for land line phone service at home. Can you believe it? We wanted to give the phone company money and could not."

"Given the fact we were creating new jobs and eager to pay taxes, Mary and I struggled with the reasons."

"Welcome to the world of Immigration" replied Andy.

"After the approvals and licenses were finally in place, we had many lessons to learn. We placed ads in the local papers for staff. About 40 women came by during the final days of renovation but disappeared with the uncompleted application form. We suspected that many could not read or write. Then ten forms came back but with various degrees of literacy. Of the ten, only two applicants were born here or had Dutch passports. The others would require us to suffer through the lengthy work permit process. We hired the two who could work immediately and resigned ourselves to working all the roles of bartender, waiter, cook, cleaner, and management. We selected three more of the best applicants and started work permit applications. Then the shit hit the fan."

"Sounds like time for another beer" announced Andy as he popped two more open and applied the lime to the top of each.

"Bloody obstacles continued which caused Mary and me to ride an emotional roller coaster. After paying for the work permits, we learned in a follow up meeting at the Labor Office that a new rule would require applicants to be off island when the permit was being processed. Imagine. People come to work in a labor market that has shortages of qualified workers but are told they need to leave the island to apply for a job. It creates an underground system and encourages law breakers instead of addressing the needs of the employment infrastructure."

"What about the two you hired who were born here?"

Tim shook his head from side to side. "We experienced immediate hurdles. Too much, too fast. The assistant cook and kitchen cleaner, a 23 year old man, presented a St. Maarten birth certificate with his application. I never noticed that his mother was from Trinidad and his father from Haiti. Born here is born here, I thought mistakenly. As it turned out, he never bothered to apply for a Dutch passport during the years he grew up on the island. Without that, he was prohibited from working even though this island was the only home he and ever known in his life. Citizenship is not *of the soil* it is *of the blood.*"

"I never knew that there was a difference. Are you saying that he was a man without a country?" asked Andy.

"Exactly. Until a government gives you the status of citizenship, you have none."

Andy looked even more surprised. "Where is John Lennon when we need him?"

"What do you mean?"

"I just thought about the words of his song *Imagine.* Now I get it. The USA government tried to deport him several times as I remember."

Tim crossed his legs and adjusted himself in the chair. "Back to my man, we had a visit from the Labor Board and were fined when he was discovered to be working illegally. It was nuts. They actually took him down to the police station with an Immigration Raid full of other undocumented workers. Luckily a former school mate on the police force recognized him at the desk and they sent him home. We are still trying to solve that one. He came to work every day, he was honest, and was friendly to customers. We are even paying him during off season hoping to clear this up and keep him."

"Born on the island and he can not work. The logic escapes me. What is left for him? The economy of crime, obviously."

"Well, hear this. The other legal employee was a woman in her mid thirties born here and in possession of the important Dutch passport. Unfortunately, on her first day she reported to work two and a half hours late. No excuse except that she and her boyfriend had been out very late and they slept all day. With basically unlimited sick days, she started calling in sick regularly about an hour after her time to clock in. In the first two months we only paid her for an average of three days a week. Thank goodness we had her on an hourly wage and not on a salary basis! Next, I found her walking out of the back door after closing with a shopping bag filled with lettuce, tomatoes, hamburgers, hamburger buns, and two bottles of rum. She explained that the expiration dates were up and that she would take them home to her children instead of throwing them out. When I asked about the rum, she started yelling at me and stormed off. I called after her and told her she was fired. To my shock, the next day I received a call from the Labor Office explaining that a complaint had been filed against me and that a hearing was ordered. It seems that I needed formal permission from the Labor Department to fire an employee."

"Humm … another great incentive to invest here!" Andy raised his bottle and the two men clinked them in a mock toast. "Keep in mind that the inmates at the prison on the island have a union and that they often go on strike."

"It got worse. Not only did I have to allow her to return to work while Labor considered my dismissal request but the boyfriend was a taxi driver. He spread the word among his friends that our bar was not a good destination for tourists from the ships who requested a clean beach with food and drink outside of town."

"How in the world did you find out?"

"I was in town on Front Street walking to the bank and heard a group of six tourists in bathing suits ask a driver for a half day trip. They wanted a beach away from town that was not crowded within a short ride complete with bathrooms, food, and drinks. The driver advised that that Oyster Pond was the only choice unless they wanted to go all the way to Orient Beach. We are half the distance of Oyster Pond. Mary cried when I told her the story."

"Well, fares are based on distance. His incentive was to sell the other beaches. And he obviously did not care about any loss of income to the Dutch side if they went to Orient Beach. Did you ever confront the taxi driver you overheard?"

"Yeh, but later. I saw no need to upset the visitors. We are all in this tourism business together. One nasty story told by six tourists back at the ship or on one of the internet travel blogs, and the effect is devastating. It is bad enough that the taxi drivers often fight over fares at the ship terminal. Much needs to be done for public relations education in a joint effort between the Tourist Bureau and the Licensing Department, in my humble opinion. We have an Association of business owners from the hospitality industry that gets it, but they do not have the power of Government Agencies."

"Did the driver even know about your bar on the beach?"

"When I found him a few days later and talked with him about the incident he blamed his information on another man ... who turned out to be the boyfriend of my fired employee, of course. He said that he was told that I over charged tourists and poured watered down drinks. Also he heard that people were complaining on the trips back to the ship about a rip off and as a consequence the tips for drivers were small ... all a complete fabrication, but powerful stuff in the fraternity of the Taxi Association."

Andy put his empty beer bottle on the window ledge and turned to face Tim. "If your wife won't return, what will you do?"

"Lose more money, I guess. It is difficult to walk away. Our house lease is up for renewal in 60 days, but the bar lease is good another 4 years. Given the money already spent on licenses, equipment, salaries, work permits, and renovations we stand to drop over $85,000 if we don't at least open this season and give it another shot."

"You didn't pay key money to get the lease?" asked Andy.

"Nope. We got lucky on that one. This building sat vacant for years before we approached the owners. They needed someone to save it before it deteriorated more from neglect. They were happy to see us and waved the extra costs. With key money costing $30,000 to $40,000 in many cases when signing a lease the out of pocket expenses would have been unbearable for the return on the investment. I am not even counting the money we lost on spoiled or missing inventory due to the slow business."

"What is the rent?"

"Five thousand per month with no utilities and no maintenance." Tim straightened in the chair. "Would you consider buying the company? Even after my tale of misfortune?"

Andy did not hesitate. "It just happens that my wife and I are no longer involved in another business that offered us residency and work permits. We need to consider options that allow us to remain on the island. Buying your company may solve this issue."

"Well, talk to me! The company has a $240,000 lease obligation remaining over the next 4 years and I need to save my marriage. Just please don't ask me to give you money to take over the headaches."

"Relax. I am not here to take advantage of you. We will make this work, Tim." Andy stood and held out his hand for the ceremonial shake of agreement.

Tim stood and the two men shook hands.

Andy asked, "After we finish discussing details and money, could you drop me off at the entrance to Orient Beach Resort? Dana has our car, and I plan to meet her there later."

"Not at all. If you save my financial ass, my marriage and take this bar off my hands, I'll drive you around the island as many times as you want."

CHAPTER 19

▼

JACK RETURNS TO ST. MARTIN

Most first time visitors to Caribbean Islands simply assume that travel from island to island is convenient and easy since major airlines maintain direct flights from key cities throughout the USA. Island to island travel can be a challenge, however. *"Just relax and enjoy the flight"* Jack thought as he adjusted himself once more in the cramped isle seat of the airplane. This trip was a time consuming experience. For his trip home, Jack Donnelley boarded a flight in Jamaica that took him to Miami. In Miami after a long lay over, Jack would board another 2 and a half hour flight that would return him to St Martin. Most of his day would be spent in travel. *If only the damn drink cart had not started at the other end of the plane.* The first leg of the trip placed him in a seat in front of a lady with a precocious 4 year old boy. The kid kicked the back of his seat and continuously sang a rhyme from some children's cartoon show. The mother buried her head in a move star rumor magazine and tuned out the child. When the flight attendant had asked for his drink order, Jack requested a bottle of scotch.

"Sir, all of our drinks are served to you in the individual small bottles."

"I know" replied Jack with a nod of his head towards the seat behind him. "I was just thinking that I might need at least 12 ounces for medical reasons."

The flight attendant did a quick appraisal of the situation and gave Jack two small bottles and a cup of ice. When he reached for his cash to pay, she interrupted his movements and leaned forward so that only Jack could hear, "On the Captain, Sir. That is his family. Just push the call button when you need more. I understand."

"Oh, must be a second family since the guy I saw walk into the cockpit earlier looked older than me."

The flight attendant only smiled politely and moved to the next seat.

Jack, my boy, stop whining. You have traveled to business conferences for years without the first seminar love affair and now you are an experienced ménage a trois participant. Suck it up and enjoy the ride. You don't have to take the little monster home, the Captain does, Lucky guy. The rest of the trip Jack kept his mouth shut and found himself counting his blessings.

During his stop and wait in Miami, Jack wondered how many of the hordes of Spanish speaking travelers were immigrants living in the USA. In the restaurant where he had lunch, everyone one of the waiters, waitresses and bus staff appeared to be of Spanish descent. He couldn't help noticing the friendly attitudes and hard work ethics. They shifted their language skills from Spanish to English so quickly he wondered which language they used for thinking private thoughts. *Perhaps both.*

He remembered a joke he was once told.

What is a person called who speaks three languages? Tri-Lingual.
What is a person called who speaks two languages? Bi-Lingual.
What is a person called who only speaks one language? A white American

Two of his European friends told him the joke at a bar on Orient Beach. He was embarrassed by the truth behind it.

When his flight from Miami to St. Martin was called for boarding, Jack walked toward the gate with a new purchase: a twenty CD collection of "Learn French" self help instructions and a portable player with fancy Bose sound blocking headphones. *You are never too old to learn new ideas, new opinions or new languages.* For this leg of the journey, Jack found himself next to an attractive young woman who had her IPod head phones plugged in once the plane was in the air and totally ignored the old guy next to her. Jack was completely relieved. No precocious children near his seat on this flight. He plugged in his new head phones and relaxed in privacy. To any other traveler passing in the isle, the retired man and young girl in seats 15A and 15B looked like they were traveling together in perfect harmony!

As the plane began its descent for a landing on St. Maarten, a male flight attendant handed Jack and the young woman Immigration cards. Jack produced his ever ready travel pen and started to complete the form as the young woman caught his eye. "When you finish, can you help me with mine? This is my first trip out of the USA. I've never had to fill out forms like this before to go to West Palm Beach or Aspen."

"Probably not." Jack chuckled and added, "No problem. Glad to help" he said as he subconsciously tucked in his stomach and straightened in the seat.

"My name is Fiorella. What is yours?" asked the dark skinned beauty with long brown hair and brown eyes.

"Jack. Nice to meet you, Fiorella. Great name. Is it Spanish?"

"Probably. I'm not sure of the origin. My mom was from Peru. Dad met her during a 3 year stint in South America and married her the first year. Since he was from the US, they returned to the States when I was only 2 so the good old USA has been my only real home. Mom emails some of her friends from school but her parents died when I was only 7, so we don't have a lot of contacts in Peru. Mom was an only child. Our family is completely US based on my father's side. When I was growing up my dad was transferred around the country several times but I seemed to fit in best in San Diego, probably because I look Mexican or South American, so I call California my home."

"I knew I heard a Valley Girl dialect in that accent."

"And you, Sir, sound like a New Yorker."

"Touché" replied Jack as he opened his passport to find the origination date and registration number for the Immigration form. Fiorella watched him then reached in her purse and pull out her USA passport.

"Jack, do you mind if I slip past you and visit the bathroom before we land?" she said standing and putting her purse, passport and form on her seat. Jack pushed up the service tray and held his paperwork while she squeezed past his knees into the isle. Her low cut jeans and cotton top separated as she moved and Jack caught a glimpse of a bold flower tattoo centered on the small of her back. Jack blushed and hoped that Fiorella had not noticed that his eyes were fixed on her.

Turning his attention back to his task at hand, Jack quickly filled out the Immigration form truthfully to indicate that he was a US citizen with a US address and a passport issued in New Orleans. He answered the questions in the negative to indicate that he was not carrying plants, foods, or over $10,000 in cash. *Does anyone ever check YES?* Then he listed his temporary St Martin address as Cap Caraibes on the French side of the island since his rental management company for the apartment was also the name of a well known Orient Beach Hotel also managed by them. *A small white lie.* He finished the form and signed it as Fiorella returned and once again brushed in front of him and gave him another wonderful view of her tattoo.

She dropped her service tray and accepted Jack's pen. He placed his form next to hers and she quickly reviewed his answers. After she opened her own passport and copied the number for the form, she laughed. "Small world, Jack! I am also staying at Cap Caraibes. One of my girl friends is getting married on Saturday so all of us in the wedding party are staying in the Orient Beach hotel. The bride and groom have a villa close by. We plan to party!"

"Actually, I rent from Cap Caraibes which is also a real estate company in the resort. My apartment is in Grand Case, a small village 10 minutes down the road."

"You LIVE in St Martin?" asked Fiorella raising her voice with some excitement. "How cool is that?"

Lowering his head to show discretion, Jack leaned closer to her ear. "Well, yes I do but not without some need to keep myself under the radar. You see, I do not have residency. I am a tourist like you. Or to be more brutal, I am a wet back just like the illegal residents in California, Texas or Florida that evoke so much public attention and criticism."

"Jack, you must be kidding. I can't imagine you running from uniformed Immigration Officers as they chase you and try to lock you up."

"Because I am American?"

"Sure. Aren't we welcomed everywhere?"

"Everybody loves tourist dollars. Come and spend money and then leave. Even small cities in Russia have a tourist plan. But no one wants new neighbors. Especially neighbors who look different then they do, sound different then they do, and have a different culture than they do. Isn't that what prejudice is all about? I don't mean to be nosey, but how old are you?"

"I am 32 years old, I have a college degree, a great executive position with an Arts funding organization, and regrettably, this is my first trip outside of the country. My boyfriend for the past 5 years was an excellent snow skier and we spent our time off in Colorado hiking, camping, or at ski lodges. My parents only vacation in Florida since my mom hates snow so I spend the Christmas Holiday there. Now I feel like you have shocked me into realizing there is a whole world that I never noticed."

"We all get busy and don't always see the struggle others face. Don't feel uninformed. Network news and the newspaper articles are full of immigration stories but most folks only skim over the parts that affect them directly. Unless you are trying to live in a foreign country, it really has no meaning. So for now, enjoy your trip, party with friends, and look for the story behind the story some other time. By the way what happened to the skier?"

"He moved out six months ago to find himself. He said he just needs some time before making a lifetime commitment. I am damn tired of sitting at home and feeling sorry for myself! So when my friend decided on an island wedding, I was the first to book a ticket. How about you, Jack? What does your wife think of island life and being illegal?"

"She died from breast cancer a few years ago. I still wear my wedding ring." Jack straightened his seat back and returned his tray to the locked position in preparation for landing.

"Oh, God. My big mouth. Now I feel so insensitive as well as naive. Please forgive me" she said softly as she took his hand and held it.

A stunning woman 20 years younger than him was holding his hand. Jack's ego momentarily soared. Then Jack remembered the older Pilot on the last flight and his young family. He shuddered. As he struggled to find an escape from her hold, the final approach to the runway was announced over the intercom system. Absent mindedly, Jack used his other hand to close her service tray and lock it. She released his hand and they prepared for landing. The plane dropped over the blue water and roared past the Sunset Beach bar for a perfect landing. The male voice on the intercom system interrupted again, "Ladies and Gentlemen ... welcome to St. Maarten. The temperature is 86 degrees and the local time is 5:30 ... one hour ahead of Eastern Standard Time."

Fiorella and Jack moved with the crowd from the plane into the Immigration greeting area. Although the plane had arrived within a few minutes of another large jet, there were only 2 open windows to clear the anxious tourists. Impatient travelers tapped their feet in line as each individual or couple stepped up to the next vacant window in anticipation of getting to the hotel or villa as quickly as possible and donning a swim suit.

When a young man moved too close to the glass enclosure behind a departing man and woman, the uniformed Immigration Officer, an over weight woman with an air of authority, boomed through the patrician, "Stay behind the yellow line!" Confused and appearing somewhat embarrassed, the young man stepped back quickly.

As each passport and completed form was carefully examined by the two Officers on duty the pounding sound of the stamp on the documents became as welcome a sound to the next in line as the impersonal summons from a bank teller after standing in line for half an hour. Jack thought, "*I served in uniform for 12 years before becoming a Detective … was I this bad? Did I consider myself this important? Probably, but I hope not.*"

Time dragged by as the two lines painfully moved forward. The tourists cleared by Immigration disappeared around the corner to collect luggage. Finally, Fiorella and Jack were next for examination. Fiorella moved quickly when called and Jack watched as she was questioned about her visit. As soon as he was allowed, Jack greeted the Immigration Officer with a friendly "Good Afternoon" and slid his passport and form under the glass opening of the cubicle in which the woman sat. She opened his passport first, compared the photo with Jack's face, and then she flipped slowly through the stamped pages.

"Do you visit us often?"

"Yes" replied Jack.

"Do you have your return ticket?"

"Not with me. I was in Jamaica for a 5 day conference, so my return ticket was to St. Martin." Jack looked directly at the lady. "When I came into the island 57 days ago, I showed by return ticket. I am scheduled to return to Miami in a month."

The Immigration Officer was unimpressed by Jack's answer. "You must have a return ticket. I am going to confiscate your passport until you return and show me the ticket."

"But I am staying on the French side. Riding home and returning with the ticket will take me two hours."

As she dismissed Jack with a wave to the side, she turned toward the waiting line and called out, "Next in line!"

Fiorella watched and waited for Jack just beyond the doors leading to luggage claim. "What was that about?"

"I screwed up. I forgot to travel with my return ticket to the USA when I left for a conference in Jamaica. She confiscated my passport until I produce the return ticket."

"You are kidding."

"Nope. I am on my way to the ticket counter for one of the small island air carriers to buy a ticket to St Thomas. Live and learn. Luckily the cost is only around $100. One of my South African friends was returning to her boat in the harbor here from a visit to Great Britain to see family when she was forced to buy a return ticket before she could board the plane in Europe. She explained that she lived aboard a boat and had transportation away from the island but they made her spend $1600 anyway."

"I had no idea" replied Fiorella with a puzzled look. Clearly her almost 30 years of living in the USA had not prepared her for international travel.

"Oh, it can be crazy. There is a story of a Mega Yacht owner who flew into Antigua on his private jet. He was going to join his family on the yacht and spend a few weeks in the Caribbean relaxing. When he tried to clear Immigration, the Officer on duty made him buy a return ticket. No amount of explaining to her that he owned a yacht that was home based there and a private plane that enabled him to fly anywhere in the world convinced her. Since his pilot had already left, he had no choice but to buy a ticket. Needless to say, he was pissed. He took his yacht out of the harbor that afternoon and vowed never to return. Can you imagine the amount of revenue lost to the island by the actions of one over zealous Immigration person?"

"Jack, why don't you go and buy that ticket to St Thomas and I will wait by the luggage claim area for your return?"

"Okay, I'll return with my ticket and two ice cold Caribbean beers!"

She cocked her head again at Jack. "Now that's the way to turn lemons into lemonade!"

Jack returned within a few minutes and handed both beers to Fiorella. She was sitting on her luggage and was watching the carousel circling with only a few pieces of luggage remaining. He waved a new ticket envelope in triumph. "Mine is a large blue roll on bag with an NYPD tag on it. Grab it if you see it go by! And don't drink all the beer." Then he disappeared again to retrieve his passport from the Immigration station.

Unfortunately the process was not any more efficient than the initial arrival clearance and Jack was gone more than half an hour. Checking her watch from time to time, Fiorella entertained herself by people watching and reading some of the free tourist magazines that advertised restaurants, casinos, attractions, and all night clubs. Another twenty minutes or so passed before she saw him turn the corner and give the touch down signal.

"Score" said Jack loudly as he raised his arms like a football official. "Oh, oh … looks like the beer is gone."

Sheepishly she raised her empty hands in surrender. "Honestly, I was almost kidnapped by a band of rejects from the Survivor Show auditions. I had to give them the beers to buy my freedom. But I think I can afford to treat you this time. Then I'll hail a taxi and be on my way to join the girls."

Haunted by the older pilot's young family on the earlier flight, Jack shook his head in agreement. It was better to let her go and join her friends. *This could be trouble.* As he pulled up his luggage and one of her bags, her big dark eyes met his. Melting, he changed his mind suddenly. In a flash, Jack imagined himself like a skydiver getting ready to jump out of a perfectly good airplane. "Fiorella, my car is in the lot across the street. Let's go have a bite to eat and then I'll drop you in Orient Beach at your hotel. It is close to my apartment and there really is no need for you to take a taxi."

"That sounds wonderful" was her immediate reply.

Jack continued to hold his stomach muscles in place as they crossed the road together toward the parking area.

CHAPTER 20

▼

GUANA BAY, TWO WEEKS AFTER ANDY FLED FROM THE POLICE

Dana was beside herself with emotion. Two weeks had passed since the police visit and there still had been no calls from Andy. For the first few days, Jack had called or stopped by daily to assure her that all was well since he was receiving calls regularly from her fugitive. It pissed off Dana royally to receive information second handedly, but Jack explained that Andy did not want Dana to be compromised should the police visit again or worse, take her in for questioning. Now Jack was off island attending some police conference in Jamaica. Dana felt abandoned. At this point, she knew nothing about her husband's hiding place or safety. *He could be lying dead in some ditch. Why won't he just talk to the police? Is he guilty? This is fucking nuts!*

With too many memories of the attack in their home and later news of the murder of Nat, she was jumpy and extremely cautious. Coby, the coconut retriever, continued to follow her from room to room. Fortunately he slept at the foot of the bed and that gave Dana a feeling of some protection. A few days ago the gardener suddenly appeared unannounced and off schedule in the front garden and the alert dog flew through the air knocking the 175 lbs. man into the dirt. Dana had to rush to his side and rescue the frightened Haitian from the growling beast. After apologizing and giving the worker an extra twenty dollars, Dana took the dog into the house and gave him a treat. Her monster was now an even greater comfort. *Andy, please get your ass home. We miss you.* She spent little time away from the house except for some occasional grocery shopping and the outside lights were always on at night. Feeling somewhat like a prisoner, her anger would shift from Nat to Andy like the ebb and flow of the ocean on the beach.

Her appetite has almost non-existent and she was afraid to have more than one glass of wine at night in case she needed her wits to defend herself. Tonight was no different, so she settled on the sofa with every light on in the house and on the outside. As she tried to pass some time with a new Perri O'Shaughnessy book, she thought, *"Come on Nina Reilly, I need some woman to woman confidence to get me through this mess. You are my role model."*

Deep in thought and momentarily distracted by the opening chapter, her cell phone rang on the side table and the unexpected sound nearly stopped her heart. Feeling the adrenalin rush, she reached for the phone and answered.

"Good afternoon. This is Dana." Although it was early evening and dark outside, the afternoon greeting was still appropriate.

"Hey Honey. It's me. Richard. Any sign of the one arm man?"

Relief flooded her emotions, a tear dropped down her face that was quickly replaced with a rise of anger. "Only when you get here and I rip off your arm and beat you to death with it."

Andy remained quiet on the other end to allow her to compose herself then quipped, "I guess a blow job is out of the question."

Raising her voice to a near scream, Dana hollered, "Are you crazy? I have been worried sick about you, I'm barricaded in this house with CoJoe, the killer dog, and you call up to play games like a college boy? Where are you? When are you coming home? When will this madness be over? I'm afraid to have more than one glass of wine incase I have to fight off an attacker. I can barely eat. I jump at every noise. I sleep in one hour segments then sit up for hours. I feel like I'm going crazy." Dana started to sob.

"Easy. I called to ask you to come and get me. The coast is clear. We are going to be alright, I promise."

"How can you be sure?"

"I just got off the phone with Jack. He is back on St. Martin from the Jamaica trip and called with great news. Trust me. I'll explain over dinner at the La Cadre Restaurant in Orient Beach. Meet me there as soon as you can. Alex has your favorite foie gras waiting for you."

"Are you nuts?"

"Well, no. But funny that you mention them. I will be the horny devil bearing a strange resemblance to a well known dashing movie star waiting for you at the bar. God, I have missed you."

"You are impossible ... I can be there in 20 minutes."

CHAPTER 21

▼

ORIENT BAY RESORT, THE SAME NIGHT

Dana and Coby walked from the parking lot in Orient Resort into Le Village d' Orient. Near the entrance to the restaurant Le Cadre, Dana looped Coby's lease over a pole and told him to sit. The dog obeyed with a whimper of protest, rested on the grounds of the courtyard then turned so that he could watch Dana as she moved through the outdoor tables on the terrace. The small area gave the dog a good view of her and he did not bark. Dana spotted her husband easily and felt the joy of a school girl on a first date.

"Hey good looking, my husband is drunk in the hotel room and I am looking for a wild ride. Would you perhaps know a good horse back riding stable in the area?" she whispered as she pulled out the bar stool and sat down next to him.

Andy stood and hugged her much too long. Alex's husband, the bartender, looked over at his favorite customers and bellowed, "Get a room, you horny Americans! No French kissing at this bar." His heavy French accent made both Andy and Dana laugh at the corny admonishment of their public display of affection.

"That was a Freedom kiss, not a French kiss!" replied Dana.

"So much for breaking the ice and cutting the tension." Andy said as he released Dana. Then he pointed to a motorcycle helmet on the stool beside him.

"I brought along a helmet just in case you tried to make good on your threat to tear off my arm and beat me to death."

Dana laughed again as the bartender placed a cold glass of chardonnay in front of her seat. "You're safe for now. I might change my mind once I hear the details of the last eight days, however. On the beach with pretty French girls, I see. And here I was worried about your sorry ass. Let's hear how you are going to beat the murder rap, Dr. Kimball."

Coby watched the reunion and strained at his leash to join them.

Andy stood and grabbed his beer. "Come over to this table near the courtyard. Coby will be able to see us better and I'll bore you with the details of my life on the lam." Andy walked towards an empty table as Dana followed. After stopping to leave his beer next to his napkin and flatware, Andy continued a few feet to pet the happy dog while Dana got settled and studied the chalk board menu.

As he returned to the table, he found Alex, the chef, chatting with Dana and showing cell phone photos of her new baby. Both women continued with their spirited conversation as Andy adjusted himself in the seat and watched his patient dog relax on the edge of the promenade. Several children passed and stopped to admire the animal, and Coby savored the attention and head rubs. On the turn of a single phone call from Jack, life had returned to normal. They were enjoying the moment, eating out under the stars and watching each other laugh again. Andy began to forget his eight days of hiding.

When Alex returned to the kitchen, Dana got down to business. "Okay, start at the beginning. How did you escape the neighborhood and the man hunt? Where did you hold up, Jesse James? How many naked women chased you while I sat at home half crazy with paranoia? At least you are wearing the clothes you left home in ... and you don't smell bad or like cheap perfume."

Andy decided to start with the housing issue. "Well, I caught a ride here and went to Carl and Lisa's condo. I knew where he hides the emergency key for use when locked out by a sudden gust of wind or an angry wife. I called them in Rhode Island and explained our situation. Carl asked me if he could send in a private plane to rescue us. You know how he is. I assured him that I would be fine and that you were safe."

"Okay. So you were safe and warm. Or cool if you put on the AC."

"Yes. I was in need of a bath and since they have a washer, I could recycle my clothes. Carl had bathing suits in the condo and I borrowed some to visit the grocery and walk around the house. I bought a few new T-shirts to blend in with tourists, too. But most of the time I was afraid to venture out very long. Then Jack called earlier tonight and the heat is off. A young woman who worked in a tourist clothing shop was found brutally murdered this afternoon and all attention has shifted. Nat's murder is what they call old news at this point. Also his business dealings, the large amounts of cash he had hidden, and a possible connection to human smuggling and organized crime makes him a low priority. Police lose their motivations when a bad guy dies. But I am glad that I stayed in hiding these past days."

"I'm supposed to believe that you stayed in the house most of the time? Sure."

"I had to. If someone saw me on the beach or at a bar and reported me to the Gendarmes, I could have been arrested. Staying out of sight avoided being picked up for questioning."

"The invisible man lives, I presume. You could have called me, you know."

Andy was sensing that Dana was getting angry again so he tried to change subjects "Dana, I bought a business for us on the island."

Momentarily stunned, Dana picked up her wine. "I think I need food. My insane husband, running from a murder investigation, stops to buy a business. This is getting wilder than my crazy, irrational fears. What in the hell did you buy, Mr. Trump? A consulting firm to help people run from the law? What is the name of your new business?"

"The Former Life Bar and Grill in Guana Bay down on the beach west of our home. And I hate to correct you, but WE now own the bar. Not me" said Andy as he ducked to his left in anticipation of a flying object to come his way from Dana's hand.

Instead, Dana looked at Andy with disbelief. She knew the history of the failed business.

"Dana, Honey, listen to me. It will be great. We can build a business that prospers. The area is perfect. It is only minutes from the tourist shopping area but far removed from the hustle and bustle. New housing is being built in our neighborhood that increases the density, the crime is low, and we can work with the market to develop a plan to bring cruise ship passengers and day visits from hotel guests. What a great opportunity!"

Anticipating their food order, Alex appeared with Dana and Andy's favorites. "On the house, you love birds. We appreciate your promotions for us. Everyone who comes here with your recommendation spends lots of money. Merci."

Andy picked at his plate and waited for his wife's next question. His stomach was beginning to hurt.

Dana enjoyed some of her favorite appetizer of foie gras with caramelized onions on a bit of crisp French bread and fumed for a short time before her fuse exploded. "So, Einstein, what is your plan for turning a pig's ear into a silk purse on this island? You must have had a vision to make you commit to this insanity without even talking to me."

Andy ignored her outburst and continued. "I met the owner of the restaurant when I fled from the house. He was so frustrated with the complications and never ending delays of island business requirements and Government paperwork procedures that he was ready to throw in the towel. Since he was facing more losses in the operation of the business and it was unlikely that his wife would return for the high season, he made us an offer that I could not refuse."

"Why do I feel that my ass is being lubricated for a great screwing? Or do I wake up with a severed horse's head in my bed tomorrow?"

"I'm ignoring that comment and going to explain" noted Andy as Alex appeared with more French bread and a bottle of wine to refill their glasses. Andy picked up the pepper mill and ground some over his beef Carpaccio. Nearby, Coby watched his owners carefully and looked concerned.

"Tell me where we got the money to buy this looser."

"I pulled twenty thousand dollars net out of my retirement account to handle all of the closing and transfer costs plus give us start up cash. The owner agreed to finance the equipment and his improvements over 3 years with payments starting six months after closing. Also I contacted the landlord and negotiated a 25% reduction in rent during the first start up year of operation. They were not blind to the problems the business was having and understood the possible loss of rent if the business simply closed."

Dana studied her husband's face.

Andy reached over the table and held her hand. "It won't be a loser, if you and I bring our management skills to develop it. Look what we did for Nat. We built his struggling business to a success and we can do it again. This time it is for us, not for an ungrateful ego manic who only wanted to line his own pockets."

Again silence over took the mood of the dinner.

Dana took another sip of wine. "Yes, and the check is in the mail. Or, how about the usual saying: I am from the Government and I am here to help you after a hurricane? Very popular in New Orleans after Katrina, I heard."

Andy knew that his wife was still not ready to join the venture. "Honey, we can do it. You can do it. I can do it. This beach bar needs a marketing plan from people with Caribbean experience. We love this island. We love these people. We just need to work with the system."

"Andy, love of my life, have you really thought this over carefully? We need employees, we need operating capital, and we need good planning so that I can sleep at night" whispered Dana.

"Chill Baby…. Sleeping without my sexy wife has made me crazy but not stupid. Eight days in isolation gave me the time to think this project through. We will focus on your concerns in our business plan. Now back to the urgency of this decision. We need to have legal status to remain on this island. Remember, with Nat dead and our business relationship kaput, we will run out of time on our work permits. Sooner or later we would have to go. This company offers us ownership of a business and the ability to remain in Paradise. Besides, the owner whose name is Tim by the way, passed me the names and numbers of several people who have come knocking looking for a job for high season. Ironically, one of them is Megan. Remember her? She worked with Nat."

Dana put her face into her hands and leaned into the table. "I should have stayed in the Army. At least by now I would have a nice retirement."

"First" Andy replied, "Forget *the **if you build it they will come*** approach to operating a beach bar. Our business plan will address the taxi drivers as sources of walk in business from the cruise ships. We will have a free family day for them to bring their wives and children to experience the food and beach amenities on a regular basis. Developing those relationships are crucial especially in the first 90 days. We need to over come some rumors and innuendoes of poor performance. Next, we will establish relationships with the Activities Desk of every hotel likely to send a tourist couple away from their property for a day at the beach. We may even consider hiring a shuttle bus to make free pick ups on a scheduled basis daily. Then, and this is where you are so talented, we will turn our attention towards inexpensive physical improvements that make the day's beach experience a pleasant one.

"Like what, Mr. Kroc, yellow arches and assembly line fast food?"

Andy reached over and held his wife's hand. "Lockers to secure valuables while on the beach for example. Outside showers for customers to refresh after a dip in the salty Caribbean water. Dressing rooms instead of smelly bathrooms for changing clothes. Just to mention a few of my ideas … learned after my years of experience of taking a Princess to the beach around the Caribbean."

After another moment of silence, the light bulb of creativity began to show on Dana face. Andy could tell that she was thinking about possibilities and operations. Several minutes passed and Andy waited for her final decision. Andy almost admitted defeat when Dana finally spoke, "I get it. I'll do it."

Relief showed immediately on Andy's face. "Thank you, Dana. You will love this project."

"Let's not forget that I want comfortable beach lounge chairs with thick pads and big umbrellas."

"Of course, but when we open on this shoe string, you are the cook. Sorry, no time for the beach, my beauty. You are in the army now. Ready to make great burgers, homemade chicken salad, and fresh roasted turkey sandwiches? All with a great twist of imagination and presentation, for sure!"

Dana picked up her wine. "I knew I should have killed you when I walked into this place."

"Don't complain. I will be the one who cleans the bathrooms every hour on busy days."

"Andy" Dana paused to munch another piece of the delicious duck flavor on the bread. "When we have it going strong and need more staff, can we hire pretty young French beach boys to set up the chairs?"

From that day forward, *The Chill Grill Restaurant* was born. The bar area would retain the Former Life theme and name because it just sounded like a good idea. Plus Andy would not give up the naked Former Porn Star mannequin. *Men and their toys* rationalized Dana.

Fantasy is good for business rationalized Andy.

Both of them were correct when it came to rationalizing. The business would grow with their management, common sense, hard work and creativity. Opening day was accomplished just before the Thanksgiving rush of high season and a small crowd of delighted visitors found a rustic wooden boat propped up next to the main entrance to the premises with the following greeting painted on the bottom:

Welcome to the Chill Grill Restaurant

Please check at the door:

Firearms
Bad attitudes
Regrets and disappointments
Demanding "I'm on vacation" behavior
Demanding "I'm a local" behavior
Dysfunctional families
Bitchy Ex-wives
Jealous or stupid Ex-husbands
Whining children (We love 'em, they taste like chicken)

And, of course, anything that might disturb our relaxed island life

All major credit cards accepted
Your dog or cat is welcome, just please take them when you leave.
No shirt, no shoes, … then you know why you're here!
Topless women drink free at the Former Life Bar when Andy bartends.

And please remember, "Chill" is our name.

CHAPTER 22

▼

PHILIPSBURG, TUESDAY NIGHT, AUGUST 19

Once he left her apartment after the stand off on her steps, Megan anticipated that Vinnie would return to his hotel or to the Greenhouse Restaurant so she turned in the opposite direction on Front Street and walked in the shadows toward the nearest Casino. Holding her purse securely with the strap over her shoulder, she kept her right hand inside where she could feel the handle of Conrad's gun just in case she was wrong and Vinnie or his fat friend stepped out to grab her. Not that she was afraid. On the contrary, her emotions of personal power were swelled when she chased off her pursuer. The confrontation and ultimate conquest offered her a chance of renewal that she had not felt since she left the Mega Yacht and Herve to remain on St. Martin.

This end of the street was less frequented by tourists, especially at night. Since the area had several low end guest houses, Caribbean men and women from smaller islands used the attractive rates to visit St Martin for shopping and gambling trips. Megan moved to the center of the street and away from the alley ways during the last two blocks. Several young men stood smoking and talking in a group ahead but did not even look up as she passed. Megan breathed a sigh of relief. Now she could release the gun and enjoy a cigarette. In the next alcove, she passed a man and woman pressed closely together in a romantic embrace. It was well known that many of the women who were gambling addicts would find an unsuspecting visitor lure them into a dark spot with the promise of sex then pick their pockets for the necessary cash to return to the Casino's activities. Worse, ten dollar blow jobs were available from the less attractive or less skilled pickpockets.

Turning into the Casino, Megan said "Good Evening" to the security Guards at the door then pushed past a small crowd of loud men as she made her way to the bar. Sitting down at the only available bar stool, Megan ordered two Tequila shots from the lady in a crisp tuxedo shirt behind the bar. When the drinks arrived, she passed the woman a ten dollar bill which was intercepted and returned to her by a young man sitting on her right side. Since he was wearing a blue blazer and white shirt, Megan immediately pegged him as another visiting businessman and not simply someone on vacation.

"My treat, pretty lady. Please put her drinks on my tab" announced the man who looked directly at Megan.

"Thank you. But not necessary" replied Megan.

With a brush of his hand, he dismissed her protest with a friendly smile and returned to a conversation with another man immediately on his right.

Megan started to leave before complications started but was greeted by a woman who took the vacated seat on her left.

"Hey Girlfriend" said the familiar voice with a strong Spanish accent. Megan recognized a Colombian friend with whom she had shared many nights waitressing at a local Italian restaurant for extra spending money.

Megan rotated immediately to face the other woman and hopefully create a barrier between her and any new conversation with the blue blazer guy. "You just finish work, Maria? That dress looks a bit fancy for slinging pizza and two dollar tips."

"No, my night off so I figured I might get lucky" laughed the woman as her eyes peered over Megan's shoulder at the blue blazer. "What are you doing out alone?"

"Conrad has to supervise security for inventory tonight. I stopped at the Greenhouse but left when two salesmen from the US started to feel me up."

"Damn. Maybe I should check'em out" Maria replied as she waved to the lady bartender. "Two lonely guys could buy my dinner and drinks all night. I'll have a BBC, please."

Megan shrugged her shoulders. "Suit yourself. But you better be ready for them to slobber all over that new dress. Also, wear two pairs of panties." She motioned for another round of tequila but kept her back to the blue blazer.

Maria reached for the frozen drink that was placed on the bar in front of her and sucked on the straw. "I did two guys once back in high school after a dance.

They were giving me a ride home and we fucked right in the back seat of the car. Not bad. One wears out and the other one pick's up where he left off."

"Jesus, Maria. What were you thinking? Guys tell everyone that you are a slut and your name is shit everywhere."

"My boyfriend was at the dance with another girl. I was pissed. I hope that he did hear all about it. Serves the bastard right." Maria pulled a cigarette out of her purse and held it without a light. "Besides, I don't give a shit what other people think. Certainly you have at least had the fantasy. Haven't you?"

Megan dodged the question. "You smoking again? I thought that you stopped."

"I did" replied Maria. "But it gives men a reason to walk up and talk. Women have to create the opportunity. Give easy to follow instructions to dumb men. Sometimes we have to lead them like sheep."

Refills from the bartender appeared for Megan and she squeezed lime on the back of her hand before gulping another drink. Her buzz was back. Or her buzz was steady. It was getting hard to tell.

"Where is that boss of yours that you're fuckin'? With a night away from Conrad you should be having fun."

Megan looked at the woman with surprise. "I don't know what you mean" she lied.

"Hell you don't. Who do you think you're kidding? We all see Nat grab your ass when Conrad turns his head. Most of the local wait staff keep away from you guys because they expect a fight to break out some night."

"Oh."

"Not that I condemn you, Girl Friend" lectured Maria. "I just wish you would share the wealth and teach lessons! I want two men fighting over me."

As the noise from the Casino continued around them, Megan fell silent and thought about Nat. He wanted her. Everyone could tell. Conrad was the problem. *I should find Nat and explain that I am leaving Conrad.* Suddenly feeling like someone who is about to miss a plane flight, Megan stood and chugged the last shot of tequila. "Got to go ... change seats with me and thank blue blazer for my drinks!"

She first walked toward the restroom but spun around at the last minute. With determination, she hurried out of the door and down the street to find Conrad's car. Fumbling around in her purse as she crossed the narrow street, she bumped the gun handle with her fingers in her search for the car key. *Damn I hope that I did not break a finger nail.* The bulk of the gun momentarily annoyed her and she debated stopping at the apartment to return the weapon to the living room coffee table. She decided that if Conrad had come home early from work, he would trap her in the house. Discarding any further delays, she knew that she had to continue on her mission to find Nat and set things right. *Nat needs me to give him the important first step. We can be together. It is up to me.*

As she drove out of town, she suddenly realized that it had been hours since Nat and Philippe left town with the two Eastern European girls. *They could be anywhere by now. What the fuck do I do? Should I go to his house? Should I cruise the Maho area and look for his SUV?* Suddenly frustrated and feeling foolish, Megan pulled over to the side of the road and cried.

Several cars passed and Megan used the headlights they cast inside her car to reach for a cigarette. As she lit the end with a butane lighter, the whole interior of her car seemed to glow as if she was under a spotlight. A truck with two men slowed and pulled beside her, but remained on the road. "Hey Baby! Need help?" came the greeting from the passenger as the driver allowed the vehicle windows to pull even with Megan's smaller and lower vehicle. Her window was down because of the lack of air conditioning and she suddenly was vulnerable. This stretch of road did not have street lights and there were few houses.

"No thanks, guys. I just needed something from my purse."

"Okay, no problem. You wanna party wid us?"

"No, I'm picking my husband up from work and I'm running late."

Both men looked at each other as the passenger rolled up his window and the truck sped off.

With her turn signal flashing, Megan pulled out behind them before another car could stop and offer help. She followed them but dropped her speed so that the distance would grow between them. After passing the entrance to Guana Bay, she realized that she was unconsciously headed toward the French side and to Nat's favorite parking spot. Her mind returned to that afternoon's memory when they stole hours away from work to drink wine and smoke pot. *Of course, why didn't I think of it. They have to take those whores somewhere if they want sex. Philippe lives on his small boat and Nat's landlord would go nuts if Nat brought home those women. The landlord and his wife have children and live in one of the apartments. No way Nat could sneak the girls in or out of the building without some type of confrontation. The guys either have to take those whores to a cheap hotel or park by the beach somewhere. And I know where.*

The road to Le Galion Beach was much bumpier than she remembered it; however, the condition of Conrad's old car was no match for Nat's newer SUV. Megan bounced on the seat as the car groaned with every pot hole and imperfection in the dirt pavement. Occasionally a large rock protruded in her path and she would swerve quickly to get around it. Throwing dirt and dust into the air made her feel like a cowboy on a bull.

I better slow down. If I wreck this piece of shit Conrad will have my ass for sure.

When she was close enough to see the first clearing, Megan pulled the car into a small alcove and turned the front around to face the road so that it would be faster to escape if a quick exit became necessary. She had never been back on this road at night, never mind alone. She killed the engine and shut off the headlights hoping that no one noticed her approach. There was a full moon tonight and walking the rest of the way would not take more than a few minutes as long as she didn't trip. *Okay Maria. Let's test your theory of pointing dumb men in the right direction for love.*

Megan misjudged the distance to the water and the parking spots that drew visitors night and day to this remote beach. It surprised her how long she had to walk. Holding her purse tightly and stepping carefully in the dark, she passed several heavily treed areas that would make perfect hiding spots for anyone seeking privacy. All were empty. Despite her caution, her sandal caught the side of a discarded beer bottle and the noise of the glass bouncing against a rock as she kicked it accidentally made her heart race. She stopped. *Jesus, I must be loony to come out here alone. What if Nat and Philippe are through drinking with the whores and are having an orgy? What do I say? Excuse me Nat, could you stop fucking that bitch and talk to me about a serious relationship? I am nuts. What was I thinking? What if they are not here? What if I stumble on a bunch of druggies using crack? Shit, stolen cars are even brought here and stripped for parts. Dudes like that would rape and kill me for sure. Fuck!*

By habit and needing to calm down, she dug into her purse in search of a cigarette and was reminded that she still had Conrad's gun. Once again, her confidence returned and she dropped the cigarette pack back into the bottom. There were many more spots ahead that could conceal a car, and she might as well have a look since she had come this far. She was going to have a look.

A few more minutes passed as she stalked every tree covered overlook, and then she saw it. *A white SUV just like Nat's.* Something was wrong. Next to the vehicle was another car. It was blue or black, but she couldn't be sure in the dark. Megan could see rental plates on the smaller car as she moved even closer without detection. Neither of the engines was running so the owners had the window down. There was a nice breeze tonight off the water and the palm trees were rustling creating enough background noise for Megan to walk without sounding any alarms to attract attention. Holding her purse closely, she moved in the dark.

Oddly, she smelled marijuana in the air but no perfume. *Where are the damn hotties? Girls like that don't go out in spike heels without cheap perfume and makeup.*

The small car was empty, but the back seat of the SUV was definitely occupied. Megan watched as a lighted joint was dropped out the window then it was followed by a beer bottle. The people in the car were moving in the seat and the whole vehicle rocked slightly. Megan heard a man's voice that sounded familiar but she could not understand all of the words from her vantage point. Slowly she moved closer and held her breath. Her heart was beating so fast that she was more afraid of dropping over dead from a heart attack than in being caught as a voyeur.

A man's head appeared in the darkness and his arms locked around the front seat head rest. "I'm on top this time" whimpered the man. "Fuck me from behind."

As she heard a second man's moan, Megan was stunned. There were no women in the car that she could see. Only two men. One was slumped on the seat while the other positioned himself on that guy's lap. Megan was familiar with the sexual position. It gave her some control to be on top of Conrad's lap facing away from him and she could vary her rhythm to please herself. But this was beyond her experience. *Two guys? What in the fuck is going on here?*

The men continued to moan and the vehicle rocked from their combined weight and movements. Confused and feeling her face redden, Megan slipped back into the foliage and dropped into a crouch. Her head began to spin and her ears were ringing. Then she passed out.

When the men finished their lovemaking, another joint was lit and the sound of more beer bottles popping and their laughter broke the quietness of the night air. Aware of new sound, Megan woke in the sandy brush to the clink of the beer bottles in a toast, but remained still. Next a door opened and one man exited the vehicle and staggered toward her. Even in the dark she could tell that he was naked. Before she could scream, he stopped and looked up. She heard the sound of urine hitting the leaves less than 8 feet from her. Then he returned to the SUV to pick up his jeans and began dressing by the open door. She could hear the other man as he slipped on his jeans while still in the back seat. There were no head liner or other courtesy lights on in the vehicle, so Megan strained to identify them in the dark shadows. The man standing outside spoke first as he buttoned his shirt. "I wish we could go somewhere nice to do this. Or even back to my boat." The English he spoke was excellent but the accent was definitely French.

The voice inside the car was now clear to Megan. "Your boat is a small hell hole. Fuck that. Someday I will have a large sailboat and we can go everywhere. I just need a few more runs and my share of the cash will buy whatever I want." It was Nat's voice.

"Couldn't you just tell your landlord that I am a family member visiting for a holiday?"

"You are cute, but you're a dumb ass. First my apartment is an efficiency and second you are French. Get it? I am not French! We can't be related. You spend the night and he will be on me like a fly on shit. He watches the place like a prison guard so that his kids will never see the real world. That afternoon you spent there with me caused me a shit storm of questions. I need my cover to make money. What kind of people do you think are supplying the Chinese? A bunch of fucking liberals? These guys are dangerous and any weakness I show could mean the end."

"Yes, but" Philippe was becoming upset. "This is a dangerous place too. Anyone could walk up and see us. We are in public! If word got out … and my father found out …"

"Then leave this all to me, sweetie. We won't get caught."

Megan could not help herself. The rage, the confusion, the feelings of inadequacy and the anger propelled her toward the SUV like a bat out of hell. "Oh yeh? Think again you assholes!" she screamed as she picked up an empty bottle and hurled it at Philippe.

The bottle bounced off Philippe's shoulder but it did not break. Terrified, the French man ran towards his car and jumped into the driver's seat while yelling in French. As the engine roared to life, he pulled away sending twigs and small rocks flying. Before Nat could exit the back seat, Megan was standing in the doorway

"Do you want a beer?" was all that Nat could say.

"Sure. Why the fuck not? I might as well toast your new love affair too. Or it's probably not new, come to think of it. I was so fucking stupid. I can't believe it. I missed all the clues. What a dumb shit I was." Megan opened her purse and took out a cigarette. Nat leaned towards her to offer a light, but she flicked her butane lighter in his face then used it to light her own smoke.

"Darlin' what are you talking about?" sneered Nat as he pulled back from her flame. "You saw two guys smoking some weed and drinking beer. Hardly an affair to remember." He relaxed in the seat and waited for the answer to his challenge.

"Okay asshole. Then why the speech about going somewhere nicer or Philippe's fear of being caught? I heard it all." countered Megan.

"Come on Megan. That is easy enough to explain. My landlord would throw my ass out on the street if he suspected drugs in his Disneyland atmosphere of an apartment building. You know that."

"Philippe is just as worried about coming out of the closet. Shit. Did you see him run? I bet he sped down that dirt road at 60 mile per hour. He was probably hoping that I could not identify him in the dark."

"Megan. Baby. You are so wrong." Nat sipped his beer and paused for the effect of casualness. "Philippe's father is out of control with anger when it comes to the crackheads in town who have broken into his store and car. You know how he views drugs. If he knew Philippe bought them regularly and even makes a few dollars on the side bringing grass from Martinique, he would surely beat him to death in public."

"You took off your clothes with another man to smoke dope?" asked Megan sarcastically. "Doesn't seem that hot to me tonight. Of course, I wasn't busy breathing heavy and having an orgasm. It must have gotten pretty warm in your back seat." She threw the cigarette on the ground and mashed the butt in disgust. "Jesus, here I was foolish enough to think we could have a future together."

Megan's relentless persistence was making Nat angry. "We didn't take off our clothes, you crazy Bitch. He may have dropped his jeans to piss in the bushes but you are mistaken. Or perhaps delusional. You must be drunk or stoned as usual. My clothes were on the whole time. You are just a stupid cunt who thinks her ass is good enough to over power and control men. Your lies tonight are not a surprise to me. Get the fuck out of my sight before I rip off your head and shit down your worthless fucking hole." The confidence in Nat's voice was real. Once again, he was able to create a reality in his own mind. "You can never hurt me. You are nothing. You and that fucking idiot of a boyfriend. Shit, I could have fucked you a hundred times and he would have stood around wondering what day it was with his finger up his ass. The guy doesn't have a clue. I think I'll have lunch with him on Wednesday and tell him what a money grubbing slut and wino whore you really are."

Megan began to shake. First the humiliation of knowing that she could never compete with the other lover, then the hostile rejection and crude attack from the man she loved, tore her soul apart. Defeated, she was adrift. Then nauseous. Unconsciously, she reached into her purse for the comfort of another cigarette but found the welcoming handle of the gun instead. Just when Nat turned slightly to his right and away from her to reach for another beer, she pressed the revolver to the back of his head and fired.

CHAPTER 23

▼

GUANA BAY IN HIGH SEASON

Probably one of the most frequently asked questions that Andy and Dana heard after the surprise from tourists of "You LIVE here? Wow. You are sooooo lucky!" was concerning their choice for a holiday vacation. "Where do you guys like to vacation since you already live in Paradise?" usually came after several rude questions of how much rent they paid or how much money they made owning a bar. Dana learned to deflect even the most inquisitive visitors by answering their questions with questions.

"We like to cruise the Caribbean or visit the States. When will you be back to visit us in St. Martin?" was Dana's standard speech.

The restaurant and bar had become a "must see" destination. Andy added a few more mannequins in the Former Life Bar when he came across an authentic WWW I leather pilot jacket and helmet on EBay and Jack donated one of his old New York Police uniforms. Dana even dug out her original Army fatigues and combat boots for display. More and more vacationing and uninhibited guests donated ball caps, T-shirts, bikini bathing suit tops and bikini underwear for the trophy wall. Most were signed and dated by the contributors who promised a return visit next year to see the exhibition as it grew in the now Former Life museum of Good Times and Outrageous Behavior. Andy installed several flat screen TV's around the bar with satellite receivers so that every conceivable request for sports or a favorite show could be met. During the off hours of non-prime time, a DVD played showing snow storms, cars and trucks sliding off of icy roads, and North American residents huddled in heavy coats on asphalt streets. It was a big hit at the bar for the bathing suit set who proudly boasted no shirt, no shoes, and warm smiles. A clothing boutique with the Former Life mantra on T-shirts were a constant sell out, and the Chill Grill logo on ball caps and ladies spaghetti tops were treasured souvenirs. After nine successful months of 7 days a week operations, the beach crowds slowed with the August preparation for back to school in the States. Andy called the staff together and announced a 4 week paid vacation as he proudly displayed the closed signs that he had printed by DeskTop publishing and made ready for posting. The first two days would allow him and his new Assistant Manager, Bob, time to store and secure the property while briefing the security service on their role during his absence. Internet security cameras were now in place with battery back ups, and Andy was comfortable that with Bob remaining on the island during the vacation both could monitor the premises with effectiveness. Bob would move into their guest house during this period and Coby could enjoy his yard during the absence of his owners.

Security and good closing procedures were important because of the large amount of cash sales during the high season. The word had spread around the island that the bar was always jammed and that business was good. It was well known among the criminal elements that the building was free standing and removed from any other businesses or homes in the area. Sensing an easy opportunity for grabbing cash, several men had either driven though the parking lot without stopping or had passed the business to case the place. This did not escape Andy's attention. Among the nautical memorabilia and former life donations he had displayed several strategically placed used baseball and ice hockey equipment items. One January night after closing, Twanda, a kitchen helper, heard a pull on the back door near the sink where she was finishing some cleaning. She checked her watch since she did not expect her husband to arrive to pick her up for another 20 minutes or more. The door rattled again, and then there was a knock.

"What cho wan?" asked the cautious woman through the closed door.

"Mr. Grandy be here?" was the reply.

"Ain't no Grandy here."

"Open da door woman. I needs to see your boss."

Dana walked into the kitchen from the office to investigate when she heard the conversation coming from what should have been an empty and quiet kitchen. "What is going on, Twanda?"

"Some mon." answered Twanda. "Don't know."

Then the door was pulled with enough force to break the wood around the simple door lock intended for daylight use. Two men stepped quickly into the kitchen and pulled the shattered door behind them. Startled, Dana gasped. One of the men was Whip. The other was definitely not the one called T-man who had tried to assault her many months before in the house. This one with light complexion and a shaved head was wearing what appeared to be a Zorro mask and carrying a machete. He looked smaller than T-man, but was in good shape and large muscles from constant workouts showed on his arms.

She ignored the masked man and concentrated on the smaller and more familiar one. "Whip. Get the fuck out of my business" commanded Dana.

The masked man turned to Whip. "Ya seen dis bitch before?"

"Yeh mon. She got some nice tits and a tight little ass" snarled Whip. "Give us the money, Bitch."

"It's in the cash drawer at the bar. I'll go get it." Dana announced to the group as she turned to walk back into the darkened dining area.

"No, we go wid you."

Twanda stood motionless and silent as Whip placed his hand on her back. "Follow the white cunt, bitch."

Dana and Twanda cleared the door from the kitchen first as the two men stepped behind them anxious to find the awaiting booty. They were so focused on the cash register at the bar across the room that neither of them saw Andy standing behind the doorway holding a baseball bat. Andy clobbered the man in the head who had the weapon, then pulled back with a low swing in time to catch Whip on the knee cap just as he turned in surprise. Whip's scream was blood curling as he dropped to the floor on top of his accomplice's body. "Aaah … Fuck mon. You crazy?"

As he picked up the machete, Andy held it high. "I bet I can chop off some motherfucker's head with this. Want to see?"

Whip's eyes widened as he tried to scoot across the floor holding his now useless and throbbing leg. "Come on, mon. Don't hurt me. Don't hurt me again, please."

Dana reached for the nearest light switch and immediately saw blood around both men. Zorro was not moving. Whip was trying to put as much distance between himself and Andy as he could, but it was easy to tell that the crawling flight was painful.

"History repeats itself" Andy proclaimed confidently as he surveyed his handiwork. "Except this time no running. We are going to beat you half to death, then drop your bodies into the sea for the sharks to eat."

."I'm kinda glad you came back to give us another shot" added Dana as she found a hockey stick. Then just for added affect, she donned a white hockey mask and let out a demonic scream as she moved menacingly toward Whip swinging.

Whip peed in his pants on the floor and cried.

The next day Andy installed dead bolt locks on all doors, reinforced the frames and jams with metal, and ordered security cameras with remote monitoring and recording to watch all possible entrances and cash register areas.

Rumors among the late night crowd spread the word that "dem crazy Americans will kill ya." Local police officers tormented known criminals in bars and whore houses with graphic descriptions of the bloody and beaten men that they had transported from the scene.

It had taken several hours for the police to arrive and escort the men to the hospital and then to jail but Andy followed the police and did not rest until the thugs were secure in a cell. Every moment that offered the opportunity, he looked into the eyes of the injured men. The remaining days of the high season passed without incident.

*   *   *   *

The island of St. Martin offers many European flavored employee benefits. All employees start with three weeks of vacation the first year. Medical insurance is covered in the Social Insurance program as are prescriptions. Socialized medicine keeps most drugs and treatments low, and there is unlimited sick leave with a doctor's note. There are twelve official Government Holidays and others, like Thanksgiving, are celebrated unofficially. Service industry employees who choose to work on Sundays or Holidays are rewarded with compensation of 200-300% of normal wages. Small businesses without enough coverage during vacation periods cope by giving everyone a vacation at once. Andy and Dana chose the slow month of September for this annual event. Once all their ducks were in a row and the business ready for the vacation closing, Andy and Dana headed to New Orleans.

After checking into the Ste. Helene, a small boutique hotel housed in a series of historic buildings on Chartres Street in the French Quarter, Dana admitted that she needed a break from success. "I'm going to sleep for 12 hours straight everyday and only eat someone else's cooking." She purred as she curled up on the big four poster antique bed. "And I intend to soak in that huge tub everyday and then do my best to screw your lights out."

Andy watched her then added, "What happened to your exercise program? I thought that walking the Quarter every day for hours starting at 7 AM was a must this trip."

"I prefer wild orgasms to exercise, thank you. Medical advice lists many benefits from sex, plus it just feels better."

Andy took off his shirt and threw it over a chair in the center of the sitting area just as someone knocked softly on the door.

Dana tensed and sat up. "No one knows we are here, except Bob."

Andy walked to the door and asked, "Who is it?"

"It's me, Johnette from the front desk. It seems that a delivery of Roses is here for you. There's a card from a Dr. Kimball. Ain't never heard of him in Naw'lens."

Andy and Dana looked directly at each other and enjoyed the reminder of his days as a fugitive. Dana joined Andy at the door, and then opened it to accept the roses.

"Oh, thank you, they're from my lover" said Dana expressing excitement and joy as she held the large vase. "They smell so good!"

The surprised woman looked at Andy standing innocently behind his wife with a puzzled look on his face. Andy raised his arms in a mock *Go figure* gesture. He handed her a five dollar tip.

Johnette acknowledged with a quick "Thank you" and spun around to leave. As soon as she heard the door shut, she shook her head as she walked away. *You see all kinds of crazy stuff in this business.*

After an afternoon of wild love making, a bottle of wine, and hot showers taken together, Andy and Dana were ready to find a courtyard café and enjoy a very late lunch. Dana dressed in one of her new cargo pants with a Chill Grill top and Andy slipped into shorts with a Chill Grill polo shirt. *Why not advertise? You are bound me meet new people.*

"Honey do I look fat in these shorts?" asked Andy.

A hair brush flew across the room and bounded off his shoulder. "Even the roses don't save you from sarcastic remarks today, Dr. Kimball."

"Ouch! Call the humane society. Your dog is hurt."

"My dog better feed me soon. Or he will learn what pain is."

Andy opened the door, "I love it when you talk dirty. That hair brush may come in handy tonight."

After a leisurely stroll on St. Louis Street to Decatur Street then along the waterfront past Jackson Square, they ducked into a small café with a nicely land-scaped garden court yard area. They stopped to admire the old brick walls, and found a table near the fountain. All during the walk, Andy carried a small digital camera and snapped away capturing the street scenes, the historic buildings and his wife's cute butt. The restaurant was no exception. He photographed the entrance and the charming seating of mismatched antique tables and chairs. He also switched to video mode to add sound to his memories. The absence of music blaring offered the soothing sound of the water falling into a small pond. The smiling hostess disappeared after handing each of them a menu. Both Andy and Dana reviewed the items with professional as well as personal interest and began debating the best way to start their Cajun and gourmet holiday away from work. A waitress approached the table and stood between their seats.

"Small world, guys. Good to see you again. Looks like your first bottle of wine is on the house!" chimed a familiar voice.

Startled, Andy and Dana looked up at the same time and saw Megan.

"Megan, what are you doing here?" asked Dana. "Good to see you again also."

"I live here now. Thank goodness." Megan explained. "After Conrad and I broke up on St. Martin the island simply got too small for me. Everywhere I went he was watching. It was freaking me out. Remember when I worked for you that month after you first opened? Every night he was waiting in the parking lot."

Andy spoke. "Yes, I actually thought that he might be planning a robbery until I recognized him from our Front Street visits. He seemed like a sick puppy to me. He insisted over and over that you had something that belonged to him, but he would never tell me what it was. Frankly, I didn't give a shit. I just wanted him to stop stalking you at work."

"Creepy. You have no idea. When I finally made the break and moved in with a girl friend he would sometimes sit in his car across the street from my window all fucking night long. Just watching the apartment. I was trapped. Funds were short and moving off the island was just too expensive for me until I could save more money. That would take time. I had to get away somehow and finally I met Steve."

Dana clapped her hands with interest. "Okay … who is Steve?"

"I met Steve at a casino one night. He works for the large casino here in New Orleans. He was actually visiting all of the casinos on the island for a work related project in layouts and security. We had a few drinks, he made me laugh, and you know …"

"Megan, you little slut" teased Dana.

"Thank goodness!" Megan agreed with a gleam in her eyes. "I'm in my early 30's and this is my first boyfriend who owns a home, has a real career, and talks about a future with me. He bought me a ticket to visit him here and I never returned to the island. Sure, I could be picked up by Immigration but then again, I wasn't legal in St. Martin either!"

Andy looked at Dana then back at Megan. "Did you apply for a Green Card?"

"Not yet. I am as illegal here as the Haitian and Dominican maids and gardeners all over the Caribbean. Steve could not get me a job at the casino because of tight controls, so a friend of his pays me under the table in cash to work here. You won't turn me in will you? So many Americans hate immigrants."

"Hardly, half of our restaurant staff is waiting for a work permit or renewal most of the time. We know the feeling." Dana answered.

"Steve is wonderful. Wonderful. Wonderful! We talk about marriage, children, and our dreams. Our future. The sex is fantastic and tender." Megan blushed.

"Just don't tell him all your secrets, Megan" interrupted Dana. "Men need to have the fantasy and mystery to keep them interested."

"Don't worry. I won't." replied Megan. She shifted from one leg to another and looked about absentmindedly.

"Can you join us for lunch?" asked Andy when he noticed that she was uncomfortable for some strange reason.

"No, sorry. I am the only waitress available for the next half hour until a new shift comes in and I still have three tables over there open."

Dana acknowledged Megan's work ethic. "We understand. Life in the restaurant biz. Tell you what, bring a bottle of Anderson's Vineyards Chardonnay with three chilled glasses and we will toast your new happiness and future with Steve."

"I can do that. I can definitely do that." Megan was now grinning from ear to ear. She hurried off on her mission. "Remember, the first bottle is on me!"

Dana closed her menu. "I'm starting with gumbo. I plan to sample it everywhere we go this trip."

"Me too. That sounds like a plan. I love you, Dana."

"And I love you Andy. Thanks for taking the first step in buying our bar. I never considered the fun we could have on the other side of the counter."

"Especially when I get to screw the cook in that small office after hours."

Dana slapped Andy playfully with her napkin. "You are such an adolescent!"

"I have an erection that is lasting over 4 hours, so call a doctor."

"Enough with the erectile dysfunction jokes. I solved that problem earlier, as I recall."

"Yes, you did. But I see New Orleans oysters on this menu. You have been warned."

They turned the pages of the menu and returned to a quiet study of the choices before them.

"Andy, did you notice that Megan was wearing large gold hoop earrings?"

"No Honey. Men look at tits and ass. We hardly ever notice freshly manicured nails, jewelry, or shoes that match the outfit. Hell, I'm lucky if I can remember if a hot honey was wearing glasses. I do, however, now notice body art. It is a part of my cultural side."

"Shit, you notice if the boobs are real or not. You are such a dog. Don't be silly. How can you be such a lecherous old man right after hot steamy sex?"

"I'm just being honest. That is all. What is your point? What did you notice that I didn't?"

Dana looked around to make sure Megan was not close to the table. Leaning over and in a soft voice she said, "Megan is only wearing one large diamond stud in her left ear just above the gold hoop earring."

"So what? Lots of women have more than one set of piercing, especially in their ears."

"Women don't usually buy single earrings. But men do. Remember Nat? He wore a single 2 carat earring in his left ear. She sure as hell never wore it when she worked for us on St. Martin in the restaurant after his death."

"And that means ... I am not following you, Dear."

"Andy, don't be such a dumb shit. Nat was found dead. The police reported it to the newspaper as a robbery and murder. His cash, his jewelry, his automobile registration and personal identification was missing. Now we see this girl wearing one diamond earring! Don't you get it? That's Nat's earring. You should call Jack."

"If she killed Nat, I should thank her. Or better yet, let's buy her a matching diamond stud to keep anyone else from becoming suspicious."

"Andy, you amaze me. You were almost thrown in jail for this murder and now you could care less if it is solved. We may be getting ready to have a glass of wine with a cold blooded killer."

"Dana, this isn't a television show or movie with all the loose ends tied up in a pretty package. Real life doesn't work that way. I read that in New York City despite all of the forensics and high tech equipment, less than half of the murders result in an arrest. Think about it. Then, of the arrests, many do not result in a conviction! There are a lot of murderers walking around out there."

"Oh God. Don't tell me that" replied Dana.

Andy reached for his wife's hand across the table. "Honey, if she did it. If she did it ... I doubt that it was a cold blooded killing. He treated people badly. Don't you believe in karma? Haven't you always heard that what goes around comes around? Weren't you angry enough to kill him at some point? I admit that I was. There was probably a waiting line to kill the worthless bastard."

Tears welled in Dana's eyes.

"Hi guys, I'm back!" announced Megan as she placed a cold bottle of chardonnay on the table with three sparkling wine glasses. Looking at them, she noticed the intimacy of the moment between the husband and wife. As she saw Dana's tears, she stepped back in embarrassment "Oh, did I walk up at a bad time? I'm sorry."

Dana wiped her tears with the cloth napkin in front of her. "No it's okay. We were just discussing buying you another diamond stud for your other ear."

EPILOGUE

▼

What drives mankind's desire to migrate? Basic demands of food, shelter, or safety may have contributed to the Nomadic experience but perhaps deep primal urges to mix genes and produce a new stronger species with each generation sparks unexplainable risk taking and exploration. In more modern times for the last few hundred years or so, the poor, the oppressed and even the powerful sought opportunity, dreams, or adventure. Then again, some content folks just stay in one place and hope to protect their world from the outsiders. Confusing for sure and probably best left to the Anthropologists and Behavioral Scientists to study and debate in an academic environment.

One thing remains constant. The process is never easy.

In a visit to Germany during his presidency, John F. Kennedy proclaimed, "I am a Berliner." One has to wonder if he understood that he would need a visa, a work permit, or a residency permit to do that in reality. Borders exist. Foreigners need to complete paperwork and be approved.

News reports tell us that approximately 400 people died entering the United States from Mexico in just one measured area in 2006. Danger is everywhere. Cold in winter, heat in summer, crime, lack of preparation, and accidents take the hopes and dreams away from those unlucky souls who fail. Yet they still migrate. They crowd into small boats and pay exorbitant amounts of money for the primitive transportation. Often while in transit they are robbed, raped, or murdered. Yet they still take the risk. Estimates when this book was written put the total number of illegal immigrants in the United States over the 12 million mark just in the work force alone. Many basic and unskilled jobs are filled by these people. On the other side of the discussion, there are positive yet unpopular aspects to the numbers. It is said that one in five college professors may be immigrants. Watching professional sports today further emphasizes the impact and importance of migrants. Many doctors are immigrants.

Ask most Americans to put a common face on typical Immigrants and you will probably listen to a stereotyped description of a dark skinned, dark haired and perhaps Spanish speaking person who has entered the country by way of a southern state's boarder or by boat on one of the many exposed shorelines. What happens when the tables are turned and the American wants to live or work in a tropical paradise? With the exception of the American Virgin Islands, US citizens become just as illegal if they fail to obtain work permits or residency. Jack Donnelly, a retired NYC police detective who is nursing the pain of losing his wife to cancer, finds himself in exactly this dilemma. Without legal residency, he makes the island paradise his new home. Who would expect that a man who has made a career of upholding laws is now avoiding them? In the USA, Megan, an attractive blonde from South Africa, could charm any diner at an American restaurant with her soft British accent. Who would be quick to condemn or judge her? Many migrants work, most pay taxes and contribute greatly to the fabric of society, but not all are welcome regardless of the country or community.

Stories of early 20th century American cities are full of discrimination against Italians, Chinese, Swedish, Japanese, Asians and others who came to fill the jobs of the growing Industrial society. In earlier times, immigrants brought against their wishes as slaves were treated much worse. However, how many would want to return to the countries of their ancestors today?

During the 2008 Presidential campaign debates a flurry of attacks were started over a discussion from a proposal in New York State to grant driver's licenses to immigrants. The public outcry caused a fire storm of media coverage. In another part of the country, a young police officer, Mexican by birth, but living and working in the USA after he assumed the identity of a dead American relative faced Federal Prison and eventual deportation because of his "crime." The human interest stories are endless and tragic. For the children of the immigrants, the challenge often places them in between two cultures. In the Caribbean, many islands deny schooling to these children. Sadly, the path to criminality often is the only choice offered them as they grow to adulthood. Perhaps one day social organizations will turn more attention to this problem. Governments can not. It is not politically popular. Follow the votes. It always leads to the money.

In 1868, Anders Gustav along with his brother Johan and his sister Sophia migrated from the family home in Sweden. Traveling through Malmo, Liverpool, Quebec and then New Jersey they chartered a course west in the new world.

Passing through Fort Wayne eventually they reached Swedona, Illinois. In 1872, Ander's wife Christina and six children joined him. By 1874, they had moved to New Windsor and their last child was born in 1876. Records are limited and dates are often contradictory. Whatever. The dumb but determined Swede made it. There are no diaries or narratives to describe the day to day challenges or the passions of the times. However, his seventh child, a son born in America lived for 43 short years and died reportedly due to a lack of available medical treatment for a simple appendicitis attack. His wife, a German Immigrant, Esther Lindorf raised their boys alone after his death and lived for over 80 years. Hers sons and descendants would prosper in America. At least one son would risk his life in World War II and in Korea. In the Swedish tradition they used the name "Anderson." During WWW II, the son serving in the US Navy would drop his middle name "Lindorf" to mask the close ties to immigration. Could Anders Gustav ever have conceived that years later a descendant of his would move to the Caribbean and start the whole process of migration over?

Somehow, he would understand.

About "Wet Feet"

The term "Wet Feet" was actually coined by those in Law Enforcement who had to conform to the 1995 revision of the Cuban Adjustment Act of 1966. During the Clinton Administration an agreement was struck with Cuba in which immigrants found at sea fleeing to the United States would be sent home. However, those who made it to dry land in the US would possibly qualify for legal residency and ultimately US Citizenship.

Basically, "dry feet" offered safety and the opportunity of a new life to those who had in many cases risked there lives to escape Cuba.

To them, "wet feet" means you are screwed.

Jack Donnelly's Travel Tips for visiting St. Martin

SXM is the airport code
The island is open for pleasure 12 months per year!

1. Pack light. You will need the room to bring home all of the stuff sold on island at remarkable prices! Ladies: 2 sundresses, shorts, bathing suits, and T-shirts. Men: shorts, bathing suits, and T-Shirts. Bring comfortable shoes and sandals. Tennis shoes are great for traveling on the airplane, and then you have them if you need them here. Plan to walk a lot in the sand barefooted. Sundresses and sexy shoes work for fine for women to dress up in the evenings. This is not like Bermuda. Men rarely wear coats and ties for dinner.

    It is always a good idea to pack a light carry on bag with essential stuff incase your checked bag is delayed. Especially if it was chilly when you left home! Wear layers on the plane and take em off when it lands. It is 86 degrees almost year round.

2. Carry ink pens with you. During the flight you will need to fill in Immigration forms listing your flight number, date of departure, your passport number, date and place of issue, hotel and other personal stuff. It is much easier to complete the paperwork on the plane with a pull down table than standing in line at the airport when you clear customs. Just keep your tickets, passport and other ID stuff handy and together at your seat on the plane.

3. On the forms for immigration, be sure to list your hotel correctly. There are few major chains, so don't rely on simply listing a well known name. If you say that you have friends on the island you may be delayed. The island welcomes tourists who come and leave. They do not welcome immigrants. You are on vacation. Vacationers who are used to traveling without showing papers are shocked. Remember all of the old classic movies with the Germans asking for "papers" and "travel documents". Play it again, Sam.

4. Relax. Everything takes a little longer on "island time".

5.   When you land in the St. Maarten airport, you will retrieve your bags in a secure area before you come out to your taxi, rental car, or ride. Do not wait inside at the luggage area for someone to find you. Taxi drivers and the public must wait out side of the secure areas.

Island information

St. Maarten/St. Martin is an island shared by two countries since 1648.

Half of the island is Dutch.

Half of the island is French.

For the French experience incase you have not been to the island before!

It is considered rude for Restaurant Staff to rush you in order to turn tables. So if the waiter comes to the table and says, "Will there be anything else?" And you say, "No, we are finished." They will let you sit and relax. This drives many Americans crazy. Most tourists want the check and they want to leave. This confuses the French. Remember that you must ask for the check! Dining is treated as one of the relaxing moments of everyone's day. Expect a long lunch and a longer dinner when you go out.

On the French side there is 220 electrical service. Leave the 110 hair dryer, appliances, etc at home! The Dutch side has 110 electrical service.

Remove batteries from sex toys and appliances before packing. Security people hate humming noises in luggage.

You will find all the comforts of home, but many products are French and European so expect that you will have some new experiences.

Getting around the island is easy, but it is most convenient with a rental car or a taxi.

Stay out late. Party. Take a taxi back to your hotel.

The cigars are Cuban.

You can feel like John F. Kennedy if you smoke a few! But you should not if you are American since it violates US law. Even some of the rums are Cuban.

Beers on the street are $1, but free in the jewelry stores. Go figure.

Yes, people drink in public on the street.

The Dutch side has gambling, adult entertainment, and all night long nightclubs.

However, they don't approve of topless women on the beach. Go figure.

The French side has no gambling casinos.

But French women are always topless on the beach.

Yes, Orient Beach is wide open when it comes to personal choices.

Some folks are naked on the far end near Club Orient. Deal with it.
Or better yet, skinny dip. You will not live forever!

Acknowledgements

It is almost impossible to thank everyone who helped with the ideas, revisions, emotional support and content of this novel but here is our first attempt:

The Daily Herald Newspaper, St. Maarten
The friendly staff at the Pasanggrahan Hotel
Detective Shaun Squyres
Elisa at Bikini Beach Bar
RT Harris, author of A Road Map for Arson
Ric Von Maur
Robert Sydney Ricks
Island 92 radio in St. Maarten
Cap Caraibes Real Estate
The Get Wet Beach Bar
Bryant Nix
Sydney Cady Drew
Mary Alice Samuelson

About the Author

B.D. Anderson

B.D. Anderson is a pen name for Bill and Debra Anderson, an American couple who decided to set aside over 20 years of successful management careers in the United States and live the dream by moving to the Caribbean Island of St. Martin in 2001. When they left the familiar surroundings of the United States to live in a foreign country, they were naive and unprepared. Only Debra had ever lived outside of USA and that was on an American Army base while she was in service in Japan. The day to day experiences as expatriates brought them in contact with many different cultures, new opportunities and challenges. The rewards and friendships they found were priceless.

As a couple they enjoy live aboard boat cruising, and they have explored many of the American and British Virgin Islands. More conventionally, they have traveled by plane to visit other Caribbean islands including Anguilla, Antigua, Barbados, Grenada, Aruba, Curacao and Trinidad. Currently they reside on Nassau in the Bahamas. Their Caribbean adventure continues …

978-0-595-48608-3
0-595-48608-8